BLOOD HUNT

Pike saw the wolves at the same time he saw Red Hawk jump through the brush. His horse was trying to shy away from the pack, so Pike dropped to the ground, pointed his rifle and fired. His blast caught the first wolf in midair, tossing its body aside.

Red Hawk took advantage of the extra time, aimed his rifle and fired. The second wolf went down.

After firing his Kentucky pistol at the attacking animals, Pike dropped it, then reversed the one-shot rifle, holding it by the barrel. The Indian did the same and they stood back to back as the killer wolves circled around them.

"We got one chance," Pike said, hefting the heavy gun like a club. Red Hawk understood and nodded his readiness.

"All right. Yell and swing hard . . . now!"

MOUNTAIN JACK PIKE

#9: BIG GUN BUSHWHACKER

JOSEPH MEEK

PINNACLE BOOKS
WINDSOR PUBLISHING CORP.

PINNACLE BOOKS

are published by

Windsor Publishing Corp.
475 Park Avenue South
New York, NY 10016

First printing: July, 1991

Printed in the United States of America

Prologue

Old One-Eye lifted his muzzle and sniffed the air carefully, finally latching onto the scent he was avidly seeking.

Food.

He trotted down the snow-covered hill, following the smell of his next meal, and the rest of the pack following behind him. They followed wherever he led them, without question. He was their unchallenged leader, and he had fought many times to maintain that title. Once, in a fight with a particularly eager opponent, he had lost his right eye. All he had there now was a scar that obliterated the eye socket completely. It was as if he had never had an eye there. Still, even with one eye, he was the king of the pack, and had not had to turn back a serious challenge in some time.

Ol' One-Eye—as he had been named by his enemy, *man*—was a huge, shambling beast with a heavy black and gray coat. The one remaining eye was a clear, sparkling gray, and he had two unusually large ears. With the single eye and the large ears, he was a particularly distinctive beast—one greatly feared by all, man and beast.

One-Eye killed for two reasons. The first was simple. He killed to eat.

The second was also simple, something that all living creatures—animal and man—were concerned with: self preservation.

He had killed cattle, horses, other wolves . . . and man, but always for one of those two reasons. He never killed a man for the first reason, because he preferred the taste of animals. Even when he killed a man he would never feed on the body. He would make sure that the man was dead, and would not harm him, and then he would go off in search of his meal. When he found his meal, and killed it, the pack stayed away and allowed their leader to feed first. Only when he was finished, and had walked away, would they fall upon the dead prey and feed themselves. They fought each other for food, but never him.

The Snake Indians, and the Nez Perce, neither a race of people who were faint of heart, called Ol' One-Eye a great god. According to their legends, the same wolf had been walking the earth for many years. It was also said that One-Eye had once brought down and killed a fully grown grizzly. They revered and respected him, prayed to him, even feared him. To kill him would be a great feat.

The white men who populated the nearby camps and settlements called him a devil.

They hated him.

They hunted him.

They tried to kill him.

They did all these things with equal futility.

Ol' One-Eye stopped now and lifted his muzzle again as the scent of mules mixed with that of horses—and of man. From his vantage point, even with his one eye, he could see a lighted camp, with men and animals.

Under normal circumstances One-Eye would not

6

have taken his pack near an occupied camp, but he was hungry, as was the pack, and so he approached, even though the scent of man was strong in the air. When the pack's stomachs rumbled, they would brave even a lighted camp if it meant food.

They approached quietly, nearly a dozen full grown male wolves following the largest, strongest of all wolves. They would make their kill, feed until they had their fill, and then return with some meat for the females, and the pups.

One-Eye halted, and the pack behind him. He saw the two men, he saw the fire—which he would instinctively avoid—and then he saw the tethered animals. Two horses, and two mules. His devious mind calculated the risk, and the rewards, and finding that the rewards far outweighed the risk, he led the pack forward.

Chapter One

"Do you know what I want?" Skins McConnell asked Jack Pike.

"Of course I know what you want."

McConnell frowned.

"What do you mean, of course?" he asked. "How could you know what I'm thinking about?"

"Skins," McConnell said, "we've been out here a month, trapping and hunting, with only each other for company. I know you, my friend, and I know what you're thinking of."

"All right," McConnell said, "if you're so smart, what am I thinking about?"

"Women."

McConnell's frown deepened.

"A lucky guess."

"Not where you're concerned," Pike said. "You're always thinking about one of two things, food and women. Since we are in the act of eating, that leaves women."

"It was still a lucky guess," Skins said. He directed his eyes out across the river, as if he refused to admit that Pike could read him so well.

They were camped near the Snake River after nearly

a month of successful hunting and trapping. Beaver may have been playing out, but there was still plenty of other game to be had. Of course, none of it was quite as valuable as beaver pelts had been, but they had decided to make do with what they had.

Pike was about to say something when the horses whinnied in unison and turned skittish. The mules followed immediately.

Pike lifted his head, as if sniffing the air, and McConnell said, "What is it?"

"I don't know," Pike said, "but whatever it is, the animals don't like the smell."

"Bear?" McConnell suggested.

"Jesus," Pike said, "I hope not. I've had enough of bears to last me a lifetime."

McConnell nodded his agreement to that. Together, they had faced more bears than they wanted to.

Pike stood up and peered out into the darkness. McConnell stood and looked the opposite way.

"I don't see anything," McConnell said.

"That don't mean there's nothing there," Pike said, picking up his Sharps. Likewise, McConnell picked up his rifle.

"Back to back," Pike said, and he and McConnell stood with their backs pressed together.

They waited that way for several minutes, just watching, waiting . . . and listening.

"I hear something," Pike said.

At that point the horses and mules started to pull against the ropes that were restraining them.

"So do they," McConnell said. "What—" he started to ask, but he never got to finish his sentence.

Suddenly, the camp was filled with gray and black shapes. Pike acted instinctively, firing his Sharps once and downing a wolf. McConnell followed, and although one of the animals yelped, it did not fall.

As the wolves charged the still tethered horses and mules, McConnell reloaded while Pike pulled his Kentucky pistol from his belt. He lifted it to fire, and then stopped. The wolves were ignoring the men, concentrating on the horses and mules, who were kicking and screaming as the wolves attacked them with teeth and claws.

One of the horses finally pulled free of his tether line and charged off with two or three wolves giving chase. The other horses—McConnell's—had already gone down, with about four wolves atop it. The mules were screaming and kicking, but Pike could see that they would soon go down, as well.

McConnell, reloaded now, stood up and aimed his rifle. Pike reached over and knocked the barrel down.

"What are you doing?" McConnell demanded.

"Right now those wolves are hungry," Pike said. "When they've finished with the animals, though, they might remember us."

"Maybe we can save—"

"There are too many of them, Skins!" Pike said. "We'd have to fire and reload, and how many times do you think they're going to let us do that?"

"What do we do, then?"

"We get the hell out of here right now," Pike said. "Grab what you can carry."

"But the horses, the skins—"

"Forget everything, Skins," Pike said. "If we don't get out of here, we'll be next."

Grudgingly, McConnell admitted to himself that Pike was right. The two men began grabbing things from their packs, watching the feeding wolves warily.

"Look," Pike said, suddenly.

"What?"

"Look!"

McConnell looked where Pike was pointing and saw

11

what he meant. One huge animal was feeding on one of the fallen mules alone. The other animals—the remaining horse and mule—were being torn apart by four or more wolves each, but the other wolf fed alone.

"Must be the leader," Pike said. "He'll feed alone."

Suddenly, as if it knew it was being talked about, the wolf looked up.

"Jesus," McConnell said.

The wolf stared at them with one eye, the other eye either gone, or never having been there. Its muzzle was dripping with blood. It stared at them, licking its muzzle clean, then looked away disdainfully and continued to feed.

"Do you know what that was?" McConnell asked.

"I know," Pike said. "Come on, let's get out of here before they finish."

As they left two wolves ran to the body of the one dead wolf and began to tear it apart.

They ran as long and as hard as they could and then stopped, crouching in the darkness.

"Do you think they'll come after us?" McConnell asked.

"I hope not," Pike said. "They should be plenty satisfied with a horse and two mules, I'd think."

"Maybe they'll run us down just for fun," McConnell said. "Or practice."

"I don't think that pack does anything for fun," Pike said. "Not considering who their leader is."

"You know, I've heard of the one-eyed wolf, but I'd never seen him before," McConnell said. "What a monster!"

"I know," Pike said. "I'm impressed, too. Did you see the way he looked at us?"

"Like he couldn't be bothered," McConnell said,

12

"and I'm glad of it. Well, what are we supposed to do now?"

"We'll have to build a fire, or freeze to death," Pike said. "What did you grab?"

"My possibles, a blanket, some bacon . . ."

"I've got the same, except I took some coffee and a pot," Pike said.

"Coffee?"

"And a pot," Pike said. Everything he had grabbed he wrapped in the blanket, and now he spilled it to the ground. "We're going to need something hot if we're going to survive. We've got a long walk to a settlement."

"What's the nearest one?" McConnell asked.

"I'm not sure," Pike said.

"Well, which way do we go?"

"In the morning we'll have a better idea of where we are," Pike said, "and then we can determine where to go. For now, let's get a fire built."

"Right."

They both looked around for something to start a fire with. There was some brush, but not enough to keep a fire going for long.

"We'll make the coffee and the bacon while the fire's burning, and then we'll just have to wrap ourselves in the blankets."

While the fire burned they boiled the coffee and held the bacon over the flame with a couple of twigs. The bacon grease made the fire flare and burn hotter, which meant it would last even less time than they anticipated. They weren't able to cook the bacon real well, but they had to get something into their stomachs.

When the coffee was ready Pike looked at McConnell and said, "Did you grab any cups?"

McConnell looked at Pike and said, "No, didn't you?"

"No."

They let the coffee sit a bit, and then passed the pot back and forth, taking sips.

"Should we leave some for later?" McConnell asked.

"It'll get cold," Pike said. "Let's get it into us now."

McConnell nodded his agreement and they continued to pass the pot back and forth until they each got a mouth full of coffee grains.

"That's it," Pike said.

As he spoke the fire flickered, and then went out.

"And that's it for the fire, too," McConnell said.

Hurriedly, they wrapped themselves in their blankets.

"Should we set a watch?" McConnell asked.

"I think we're both going to need all the rest we can get," Pike said. "Besides, if they find us there won't be much we can do about it, will there?"

"I guess not."

"Besides that," Pike said, huddling into his blanket, "we'll probably freeze to death before they can find us."

By morning they had moved together for more warmth—without realizing it, of course. Pike woke first and rolled away from his friend. Not that McConnell would have been embarrassed, not after having once spent the night together in the belly of a bear.

Pike flexed his stiff fingers and rubbed his cold hands together.

"Come on, Skins," he said, nudging his partner.

McConnell moaned and rolled over.

"I'm frozen."

"If you don't get up and move around," Pike warned, "you will be. Come on."

14

McConnell sat up and used a hand from Pike to get to his feet.

"Shit," he said, stamping his feet, "what the hell are we gonna do now?"

Pike looked up at the sky, and then at his surroundings. Neither man would have liked to admit it, but in their flight from their wolf-infested camp the night before they had managed to get themselves lost in a moonless dark. Now, with the morning light, Pike was able to see where they had run to—and where they had to go.

"We're going to have to head for Fort Hall," Pike said. "We could probably walk it in three days."

"Three days?"

Pike shrugged and added, "well, we might come to a settlement between here and there. We've stayed pretty much from our more usual haunts."

"We had to find some good hunting, Pike," McConnell said. It was his idea for them to follow the Snake River, hunt near it and explore its tributaries.

"I know, and I agreed to it, Skins, so don't go getting insulted." Pike turned and pointed. "By my reckoning, Fort Hall is about three days' walk . . . that way."

McConnell looked "that way," and then gave his friend a dubious look.

"Walk? Without supplies?"

"Well," Pike said, "I did have another idea—before we start walking toward the Fort, that is."

"And what's that?"

"We walk back to our camp."

"Back to where we ran from?"

"Why not?" Pike asked. "The wolves are sure to be gone by now, and there was one horse that broke its tether and ran off."

"They probably ran it down."

15

"And maybe they didn't," Pike said. "Let's walk back there and see what we can salvage. Maybe we can make the walk to Fort Hall a little easier."

McConnell looked back the way they had run the night before and shuddered.

"I don't relish meeting up with ol' One-Eye and his pack again."

"Neither do I," Pike said, "but let's do it, anyway."

"Hell," McConnell said, "why not? What's a couple of wolves between friends?"

They walked back to their late campsite and viewed the carnage. The horse and mules had been ravaged until nothing was left but bones and intestines. The carcasses were covered with flies. There was also a wolf carcass, which Pike had killed and the other wolves had ravaged.

"What the hell—" McConnell said.

Apparently, after feeding, the wolves had gone through the camp and destroyed everything they could.

"I've heard of wolves attacking animals," Pike said, "and men, but I never heard of them attacking the actual camp."

McConnell was already walking through the camp to see what he could salvage.

"They got most of the bacon and biscuits," he said, kicking over some saddlebag, "but they couldn't do much with the coffee."

"We can hunt for food," Pike said. "The coffee'll keep us warm. What about cups?"

"They're here," McConnell said, picking up two tin cups.

Pike picked up a set of saddlebags and found his extra shirt.

"Powder," McConnell said, "we got powder."

"Powder and coffee'll get us to the Fort," Pike said, "along with whatever meat we hunt up."

McConnell came over and stood next to Pike.

"A horse would get us there even faster."

"Ah, fast don't really matter," Pike said, "as long as we get there."

"Yeah," McConnell said, looking around them warily. "I'd suggest we get moving before they come back."

"A good suggestion," Pike said. "Let's pack what we can carry and do it."

They pushed themselves, walking a full day before they camped and made coffee. This time they found enough material to keep a fire going, and basked in its warmth and light.

"This time last night I didn't think we'd be comfortable at this time this night," McConnell said, shaking his head.

"Well, let's not get too comfortable," Pike said. "There are still wolves, and Indians to deal with."

"After those wolves," McConnell said, "I'd welcome a little skirmish with some Indians."

"What's your pleasure? Snake?" Pike asked. "Or Nez Perce?"

"Never mind," McConnell said. "I'll take the first watch."

Sometime later Pike woke up, just before McConnell started to shake him.

"What?" he said.

"I hear something."

"So do I," Pike said, standing up. He picked up his Sharps and stood stock still, listening. McConnell

17

knew that his friend had the better ears, so he remained silent and let Pike listen.

"Not wolves," Pike said. "It sounds like . . . a horse."

"Maybe it's somebody with some bacon," McConnell said, hopefully.

Now they could both hear the sound of a horse walking.

"There," Pike said, pointing.

They watched as a lone horse, bareback, came walking into camp, stopped and stared at them.

"That's my horse," Pike said.

"Well, I'll be damned," McConnell said.

"He must have smelled the camp and found us. He's probably been wandering around since last night."

They walked over to the horse, who stood quietly while they examined him.

"Not a mark on him," Pike said. "He must have outrun those wolves."

"Well," McConnell said, "now we've got a horse, we can get to the Fort faster."

"We ride this animal double," Pike said, "and we're going to ride him into the ground."

"What do you suggest?"

"We'll take turns," Pike said, "one walking, one riding. We may not get there any faster, but we'll be in better shape when we do get there."

"Let's tie him off so he doesn't wander off," McConnell said, "and then get some rest."

"I'll take the watch now," Pike said. "I'll wake you at first light, and we can get moving."

"All right."

Pike tied the horse off and McConnell settled himself down for the night.

As Pike was pouring himself a cup of coffee McConnell sat up and said, "You know what's been bothering me since this morning?"

"What?"

"Our skins."

"What about them?"

"Where are they?"

Pike paused a moment, and then said, "I never thought of that."

"Why would a pack of wolves haul off a bunch of skins?" McConnell asked. "There's no meat."

"I don't know."

"And if they didn't take the skins," McConnell went on, "who did?"

"I don't know that, either," Pike said, "but let's not worry about it now."

"But we did all that work—"

"Go to sleep, Skins," Pike said. "We need to get an early start in the morning."

"I know, I know," McConnell said, lying down, "it just irks me, is all."

As Pike sipped his coffee he decided that it irked him too, now that his friend had brought it up.

What *had* happened to all those skins?

Ol' One-Eye knew his enemy when he saw him, and he also knew where a good meal had come from. He watched the two men for a full day as they walked west, and even as the lone horse entered their camp, yet he did not make a move against them.

There was a half moon this night, as he watched the two men in their camp, and the light reflected off his silver/gray hide. Beneath the hair great muscles flexed as the animal moved back and forth. The rest of the pack had been left farther behind, but they would follow the scent of their leader, who could move more swiftly without them.

One-Eye was on the trail of the two men, knowing

that they would lead him, and his pack, to more good feeding, as they had several nights before. The pack probably would have rushed down and killed the men and the horse, but One-Eye was too smart, too devious for that.

He simply watched, and followed, until the right time.

Chapter Two

A day and a half later they walked and rode into Fort Hall, which was a fair-sized settlement made up of both wooden structures and tents. Neither Pike nor McConnell, however, had ever been there before. Fort Hall was a little bit west of where they usually roamed.

Looking bedraggled, Pike and McConnell attracted a lot of attention as they walked down the muddy main strip of Fort Hall.

Their needs were many, now that they had arrived. In no particular order they needed a bath, a meal, a drink, a bed, a woman, and then they needed to reoutfit.

"There's the trading post," McConnell said.

"That can be our last stop," Pike said. "I need to get cleaned up."

"I need a woman."

"A woman is not going to look at you until you get cleaned up," Pike said.

"Okay, so we get cleaned up. I wonder if this place has anything resembling a hotel."

"Let's ask," Pike said.

They stopped the first man they encountered and asked him if there was a hotel.

"North of the settlement there are some tents set up,"

the man said. "They're for rent, if you've a mind to sleep inside."

"What about bath facilities?"

The man grinned and said, "You can get a bath the same place you can get a woman, over at Miss Rachel's."

"Miss Rachel's," McConnell said, grinning at Pike. "I like the sound of that."

"I knew you would," Pike said. To the man he said, "Much obliged."

They walked the horse to the north end of town and found the man who was renting the tents.

"I got small tents, for one man, and I got bigger ones," the man said. He was a big man, both tall and wide, with a huge girth that almost swayed when he moved.

"Let's take two small ones," McConnell said. "That way one of us won't be bothering the other's sleep."

"Yeah," Pike said, "I know why you want a small tent, Skins."

They paid the man for two days and he gave them directions to their tents, which were ten feet apart. In fact, all of the tents for rent were set up ten feet apart. The area almost had the look of an army camp. They also paid the man to care for their horse, and handed the animal over to him.

There were small campfires outside the other tents, and men sitting around some of them. As Pike and McConnell walked to their tents, they were the object of all attention.

When they reached their tents they stowed whatever gear they had left, and then met again outside.

"When the man said small, he meant small," McConnell said. "There's not even any room to stand up."

"You don't have any intention of standing up in that

22

tent, anyway, so stop complaining," Pike said. "Just imagine how small the tent would seem if you were my size."

"Well, at least we've got some place to sleep," McConnell said, "now what we need is a drink and a meal."

"I need a bath first," Pike said.

"Then let's go and find Miss Rachel's," McConnell said. "Maybe we can get most of what we need there."

"Most of what you need . . ."

Jean Windham looked at the plate in front of her twelve-year-old boy, Barry, and shook her head. The steak she had cooked so carefully and placed there was only half consumed, but the vegetables were hardly touched at all.

"Barry—"

"Aw, Mom," young Barry said, "you know I don't like vegetables."

"I know you're not going to grow up tall if you don't eat them."

"You been telling me that for years, and look at me," the boy said.

His mother shook her head. Her twelve-year-old boy had grown by leaps and bounds, even though he hadn't been eating his vegetables, and she couldn't argue with that. The boy was almost taller than she was, and given another summer, he would be.

At thirty-eight, Jean Windham had been raising her son alone for more than five years, since wolves had killed her husband. The older Barry got, the more like his father he got, and the harder he was to control.

"I got to go out, Mom," Barry said.

"All right, but only for another hour."

"Mom—"

"Or else you can stay inside now."

"All right," Barry said, pushing his chair back, "one hour."

Jean walked him to the door and watched him walk down the steps. As she opened the door two men were walking by, and one of them caught both her eye and Barry's. He was possibly the tallest man either of them had ever seen, with the widest shoulders they'd ever seen.

"Wow, Mom," Barry said, in awe.

The boy spoke loudly, and both men looked in their direction, and the big man nodded to them.

"Look how big he is," Barry said to his mother.

"Yes," Jean Windham said, feeling the quickening of her pulse, "and I'll bet you he ate all his vegetables when he was growing up."

"Did you see that?" Pike asked.

"The woman and the boy? I saw them."

"A handsome woman, and a good looking lad," Pike said. Both woman and boy had the same hair color, an almost white-blond, and were obviously mother and son, and a mighty fine looking pair. Also, the smells coming from the house had set Pike's stomach growling. If he was any judge of odors, the woman was a good cook, as well.

This was one of those rare moments when Pike thought about what it might be like to have a wife, and a child, and a home like that one. He thought that the man who was the woman's husband and the boy's father was probably a very lucky man.

McConnell stopped someone along the way and asked where Miss Rachel's was. They were given directions to a large tent, and when they entered they

24

saw that the interior of the tent had been partitioned off into sections.

As they entered a woman in her forties approached. She wore a wrap that covered her from head to toe, which was just as well, because she was possibly the fattest woman either of them had ever seen. They both wondered if she had ever been a successful whore, as most madams they had met in the past had been.

"Can I help you fellas?" she asked. "I'm Miss Rachel."

"Yes," Pike said, "we're interested in a bath."

"Together, or separate?" she asked.

"What?" McConnell said.

"You get used to odd requests in this business," she said. "Anyway, I was just kiddin'. A bath, you say?"

"He's interested in a bath," McConnell said, "I'm interested in a bath, and . . ."

"Ah," she said. "Baths are cheap, but the and . . . that's gonna cost."

"I'll just take the bath," Pike said.

"Maria!" the woman shouted.

A dark-haired woman appeared from behind a partition. She was small, in her twenties, and well formed. The only thing that marred her appearance was a vicious scar that travelled the length of her left cheek. The way she was dressed—a shirt and trousers—it was obvious she was not one of Rachel's whores.

"Yes?"

"Draw two baths . . ." She looked at Pike and McConnell and said, "Hot or cold?"

"Hot," Pike said, and McConnell nodded.

"Two hot baths," the woman said to the girl, Maria. "Two private baths."

"Okay, Miss Rachel."

25

As Maria went off to set up the baths Miss Rachel settled price with the two of them and they handed over their money.

"If you decide you want more than a bath," she said to Pike, "we can settle up after."

"Fair enough."

"Mathilda!"

Another woman appeared, and she was obviously one of Miss Rachel's girls. The clothing she wore exposed all of her legs, and the swollen tops of her breasts. Her hair was red, long and perfumed, and she was tall enough to carry her impressively sized breasts.

"Mathilda will see to you," Rachel said to McConnell. "Just follow her."

"With pleasure," McConnell said. He grinned at Pike and then followed Mathilda.

"Maria will be along for you," Rachel said. "Enjoy your bath."

"Thank you."

Pike had to wait only a minute before Maria reappeared and beckoned to him. He followed her, noting from behind how well formed she was. He wondered if it was only the scar on her face that kept her from being one of the whores. Walking behind her he also noticed how small she really was. At six-four, he towered more than a foot over her.

She led him to a partitioned area where a bathtub awaited him. The water was steaming, and he was anxious to undress and lower himself into it.

He turned and saw that she was not leaving.

"Are you staying?"

"You'll need someone to scrub your back."

"I think I can manage."

"It's included in the price," she said, shrugging.

"Well, all right, then," he said, and undressed in front of her. When he was naked he walked over to the

26

tub, stepped into it and lowered himself into the water. He was a big man, and the tub was not exactly built to fit, so he had to hang his feet over the edge, but most of him was still submerged.

"Here is your soap," she said, coming up alongside the tub and handing it to him.

"Thank you."

She certainly didn't seem shy around naked men, that was for sure.

He soaped himself slowly, enjoying the way the heat of the water was baking away his aches. Pike had a habit of bathing in cold river or lake water whenever he got the chance. An occasional hot bath was enjoyable.

"If you sit forward," she said, "I'll do your back."

"All right."

He leaned forward and was surprised when she unbuttoned her shirt and removed it. Was it because she didn't want it to get wet, or was this included in the price, too? Probably the former. Miss Rachel didn't seem the kind who would throw this in for the price, and Maria herself maintained a bored expression, even when she was naked to the waist.

Her breasts were small, but they were firm or, to be more precise, hard. They looked like two small peaches, or peach sized stones.

She knelt next to the tub, took the soap from him and began to soap his back. Occasionally, one of her breasts would brush against him, or jab him while she was washing him, but he was sure that was accidental. It did tell him, though, that her breasts were indeed as firm and hard as they looked. It was that kind of taut firmness that only a small breasted woman could have. It was the appeal of a small breasted woman, just as the appeal of a big breasted woman was the way they swayed when she moved, or gave when you squeezed them.

After she had done his back she proceeded to his shoulders. He closed his eyes, enjoying the strength in her small hands as she kneaded the tension from him.

When she was finished she started to withdraw, but he took hold of her arm and pulled her around so he could look at her. He looked at her breasts, pale and hard, with dark brown nipples that were distended, and then looked into her eyes.

"Please," she said, "I'm not one of the girls . . ."

He examined her face. If not for the scar she would have been more than pretty, but even with the scar he found her attractive, arresting, with a full mouth and blue eyes. Her hair was dark and long, and the wet ends plastered themselves to her wet flesh.

He reached out, as if his hand had a life of its own, to touch her breast and she said again, "Please . . ."

He stopped, then released her.

"I'd like to soak a while," he said, as she stood up.

"All right."

"Just leave the towel where I can get at it and go."

She stared at him for a moment. He wondered what she was thinking. He knew what he was thinking, how nice it would be for him to pull her into the tub with him and run his mouth over those hard breasts. Suddenly, he had a raging erection and he knew that she could see it. She stared at it, then looked him in the eyes.

"Would you like one of the girls?" she asked.

"No," he said. "Just get me a towel and get out."

She turned, got him a towel from a pile on a chair, and placed it near the tub. Then she looked at him one more time, and left him there.

By this time he knew that McConnell and Mathilda would be splashing around together in the tub. For some reason he was angry at Maria, and at himself. He set his head back so that the back of his neck rested

28

against the rim of the tub, and settled in to await the cooling of the water. He was also waiting for his damned erection to go down.

After their baths they met out in front of Miss Rachel's.

"Damn, but I'm hungry," McConnell said.

"So am I."

"Did you . . ."

"No, I didn't work up an appetite the way you did," Pike said, "but I'm hungry, anyway."

"Mathilda told me that the trading post was where we could get a drink, and a meal."

"A good meal?"

"A hot meal."

"Right now," Pike said, "I'll settle for that."

"So will I," McConnell said.

On the way to the trading post Pike found himself thinking about two women; Maria, and the taller, blonde woman with the child he had seen in the house.

Chapter Three

Jean Windham was thinking about the man she had seen earlier that evening. She had not seen him in Fort Hall before, so she assumed that he must have just arrived. Lingering over a cup of coffee while she waited for Barry to return home, she wondered who the man was and what he was doing here. Her curiosity after one brief look at the man surprised her. It had been five years since her husband died, and not once during those years had she become curious about a man. Plenty of men had tried to arouse her interest and curiosity, but none had succeeded.

Now this man walks past the house, and suddenly she's curious.

The feelings and emotions that were running through her were so foreign to her that she did not even know what to do about them.

Barry Windham was on his way home, knowing he was late, and knowing that he was going to have some explaining to do. He'd been playing with some of the other kids and had wandered away from his house. As he was walking past the trading post he saw the two men he and his mother had seen earlier. He stopped dead in his tracks and stared openly at the big man.

Pike and McConnell were on their way to the trading post to see what they could do about both their hunger and thirst, when Pike saw the blond haired boy he'd seen earlier, with the woman. This time the boy was alone, and he was gaping at Pike.

"You go on ahead," Pike said to McConnell. "I'll catch up."

"What?" McConnell saw the boy then, and nodded to himself. "All right. I'll meet you inside. I'll order you a steak."

"Fine."

As McConnell continued on, Pike stopped near the boy, who was now craning his neck to look up at Pike.

"Hello, boy."

"Hello, sir."

"What's your name?"

"Barry."

"Barry what?"

"Barry Windham."

"I saw you earlier today, didn't I?"

"Yes sir."

"With your mother?"

"Yes sir."

"Was that your house?"

"Yes sir."

"A fine house."

"My daddy built it."

"You should be proud of your daddy."

"I am, sir," the boy said, "but he was killed five years ago."

"I'm sorry to hear that," Pike said. "Just you and your mom, is it?"

"Yes sir."

"What is it about me you find so curious, boy?"

"Sir," the boy said, politely, "I ain't never seen a man so big."

"Is that a fact?"

"Yes, sir, it is. Can I ask you something?"

"Go ahead."

"My mom says you got so big because you ate all your vegetables when you was my age. Is that true?"

Pike took only a moment to decide his answer. If he told the boy anything else, his mother would likely come looking for him with an axe handle.

"Your mother is dead right, boy," Pike said. "I ate every vegetable I could, and I still do."

The boy made a face, as if he had just bitten into something sour.

"Even the green ones?"

Pike bent over and said, "Especially the green ones, son."

"Golly," the boy said.

"You on your way home?"

"Yes sir."

Pike gave the boy an amused look and asked, "Are you late?"

The boy lowered his eyes and said, "Yes sir."

"Well, you best get on home and take your licking like a man."

"Aw, my mom won't give me a lickin'."

"She won't?"

"No sir, but she'll give me a talkin' to, that's for sure."

"Well, you go on home and take it, and you tell your mother you're sorry you're late. Understand?"

"Yes sir."

"Now git!"

The boy started running, then stopped and shouted, "What's your name, sir?"

"Pike," Pike called after him, "and stop calling me sir!"

"Yes sir!" the boy shouted, and turned and ran.

Pike laughed to himself, and then continued on to the trading post.

". . . and he told me that he got to be so big by eating all his vegetables." Barry was breathless when he finally finished telling his mother about his conversation with Pike.

"Is that supposed to be your excuse for being late, young man?"

"No, really, Mom," Barry said, "that's what he tol'-me—"

"Barry, I think you'd better go to your—"

"Mom," Barry said quickly, "can I have some vegetables?"

Jean couldn't believe her ears. Either her son was even smarter than she thought, or this man Pike had done something that she had been unable to do for years.

"Sit at the table, Barry," Jean said, "and I'll bring you some vegetables."

When Pike entered the trading post he saw McConnell seated at one of four tables. Apparently, the trading post counter doubled as a bar, and the clerk as a bartender. In all probability, the man behind the counter was also the owner.

McConnell had two beers on the table already, and beckoned to Pike.

"The beer is cold and there are two steaks on the way, as well," McConnell said.

Pike sat down and tried the beer. It *was* cold, and he

34

downed half of the mug before coming up for air.

"Ah, I needed that."

"What was going on outside?" McConnell asked.

"Just making a new friend," Pike said. "Barry Windham."

"Is that the boy we saw earlier?"

"Yes."

"Now that you've made friends with him, is the mother next?"

"Skins," Pike said, "you really do have a one track mind, don't you?"

McConnell suspended his answer as the clerk/bartender was on his way over with two plates.

"How's the beer, gents?"

"Cold," McConnell said.

"It's just what we needed," Pike said, "and so are those."

"Tough time?" the man asked, putting the steaks in front of them.

"Only if you call being chased by a pack of wolves tough," McConnell said.

"Wolves?" the man asked, his look turning serious. "Listen, boys, my name is Andrew Locke. I own this trading post, which doubles as the saloon hereabouts, but I'm also booshway around here. Would you mind if I sat and joined you for a spell?"

"No, come ahead," Pike said, "as long as you don't mind if we go on eating and drinking."

"In fact," Locke said, "let me get you two more beers—on me—and one for myself before I sit."

"I never turn down a free beer," McConnell said. "My name's Skins McConnell, and this here is Jack Pike."

"I'll be right back."

As Locke went behind the counter McConnell said, "What do you suppose is on his mind?"

35

"Wolves, probably," Pike said. "He seemed real interested when you mentioned them. Let's see what he has to say."

Locke had to take care of a couple of customers at the counter, but when he was done there was no one else in the place, so he returned to their table with three beers and sat down.

Locke was a man in his forties, not particularly tall, but well built, with a streak of shocking white through his salt-and-pepper hair.

"I'm real interested in what you have to say about these wolves," Locke said. "You see, we've been having some wolf problems."

"What kind of problems?"

"Well, we've had to keep our children close to the settlement, and our livestock. We lost some beef over the past few weeks, and we've had two men killed."

"By a pack?" Pike asked.

"That's right."

"Is this unusual for this area?"

"Wolves are not," Locke said. "We've had several deaths over the ten years we've been established here, but recently a particularly vicious pack seems to have come into the area—led by a particularly vicious wolf."

"Ol' One-Eye?"

Some of the color drained from Locke's face.

"The one-eyed wolf has been a legend around here even since before we came along, but yes, he seems to be the leader of this particular pack." Locke took a long drink from his mug and then stammered, "D-did you actually see him?"

"Oh, we saw him, all right," McConnell said. "He and his pack came right into our camp, bold as brass. They killed one horse and two mules, and proceeded to tear up the camp."

"How is it you escaped?"

"They were hungry," Pike said, "and so intent on feeding that they literally ignored us, and—well, to be honest, we just ran."

"I don't blame you," Locke said. "I've seen the handiwork of this pack. Where were you when this attack took place?"

"We were three days' walk from here. I guess you'd make that a day, day-and-a-half ride," Pike said.

"That's kind of far from here," Locke said, rubbing his jaw. "Maybe it wasn't the same pack."

"Maybe we just encountered them on their way away from here," Pike said. "Maybe you won't have any more trouble from them."

"That would be a blessing, if it was true," Locke said. "That pack sure has brought us a lot of grief."

"Have you had trouble with One-Eye before?" Pike asked Locke.

"Like I said, over the years we've lost a man or two to wolves. About five years ago we lost a fella by the name of Kendall Windham. His boy was with him, and claims that his father was killed by a one-eyed wolf."

"The boy saw it?" Pike asked. "I mean, he saw his father killed?"

"That's his story."

"You don't believe him?"

"The boy was—oh, I guess about seven at the time, and he was terrified. When we found the body, it had been ravaged by what had to be a pack of wolves, and not just one. Still, the boy insisted that he saw the one-eyed wolf, and still insists to this day."

"Would the boy's name be Barry? With white-blond hair?" Pike asked.

"That's him. Do you know him?"

"Is that our new friend?" McConnell asked.

Pike nodded to McConnell and said to Locke, "I met the boy today. He didn't strike me as a liar."

"I never said he lied," Locke said. "I only said he was seven at the time, and terrified. Maybe he didn't see what he thought he saw. His mother's name is Jean, and she's raised him alone since then. Done a fine job, too."

"We saw her with him earlier."

"She's a fine woman, and she won't allow the subject to be raised with the boy ever again."

"Well, hopefully it won't have to come to that," Pike said. "With any luck, One-Eye and his pack were headed for greener pastures."

The door opened then and a couple of customers walked in.

"Got to get to work," Locke said, standing up. "Glad to have met you gents. I'm also glad you were able to get away from that pack unharmed."

"Well, they were pretty much unharmed, too," McConnell said. "Pike killed one, and I wounded one, but that was all we had time for."

"You boys did the right thing gettin' out when you did," Locke said. "Come back in here anytime, and the second beer's on the house."

"You got a deal," McConnell said.

As Locke went back to the counter to tend to his trading post business McConnell said, "We gonna be around long enough to come in again and cash in on that kind offer?"

Pike thought a moment, about wolves, and about the boy and his mother, and said, "Ain't no reason to rush off, is there?"

"Not that I can see."

"Then I guess we'll stick around . . . for a spell."

Ol' One-Eye looked down at the settlement from a high peak. The rest of the pack had caught up to him and were milling about farther down. They had found some fine feeding around this settlement for a while, and then One-Eye had taken them east. That was when they ran into Pike and McConnell. Having followed the two men back here, One-Eye was thinking that maybe there was still some fine feeding to be had around here.

He narrowed his one eye and lifted his muzzle to the air.

Chapter Four

After they finished eating McConnell was in favor of a return visit to Miss Rachel's.

"That Mathilda . . ." he said.

"I'm going back to my tent," Pike said. "I'm a little tuckered after all that walking."

"You know what your problem is?"

"No," Pike said, "but you're going to tell me, aren't you?"

"If your friends can't tell you, who can?" McConnell said.

"What's wrong with me?"

"You're gettin' old, Pike," McConnell said. "It's a sad thing to see."

"Let's not forget one thing," Pike said.

"What's that?"

"You're two years older than I am."

"Yeah," McConnell said, "but I don't feel it."

"You go your way," Pike suggested, "and I'll go mine . . ."

McConnell gave Pike a little salute and started toward Miss Rachel's.

To get back to the tents, Pike had to walk past the Windham house . . .

Jean Windham was looking out her window when she saw the big man—Pike, Barry had called him—walking by the house. She started for the door three different times before she finally got to it and opened it. By that time he was almost by the house.

"Excuse me!" she shouted.

Pike stopped at the sound of her voice and turned around. When he saw her he turned and took several steps toward her.

"Are you speaking to me?" he asked, which was a stupid question because there was no one else around for hundreds of yards. The house had been built—deliberately so—away from the rest of the settlement.

"Yes, I am. Is your name Pike?"

"Yes, Ma'am."

She stepped down off the porch and he took several more steps toward her. This close he could see that she was much more than handsome. Her hair was so light that it almost seemed as if she had no eyebrows or eyelashes, but that gave her face a sort of scrubbed clean, fresh look. She would always look as if she had just stepped from a bath, her skin almost glowing. There was even some down on her arms which, in the sunlight, made her arms look as if they were shining.

"My name is Jean Windham," she said. "I believe you met my son earlier today."

"Barry," Pike said, nodding. "He seems like a fine boy, Mrs. Windham."

"Well, I wanted to thank you . . ."

"For what?"

"For whatever you said to him today," she said, rubbing the palms of her hands nervously on her thighs. She was wearing a simple dress which did nothing to hide the sturdy look of her body. She had

42

solid breasts, hips and thighs which Pike couldn't help but admire, while trying hard not to stare.

"What I said?" he repeated, frowning.

"He came home and asked me to make him some vegetables."

"Oh, that!" he said. "Well, you started that by telling him I grew so big by eating them. When he asked me if you were right, I just said yes."

"Well, I thank you for it," she said. "I've never seen him eat so many vegetables in one sitting."

"Even the green ones?" he asked.

She laughed, tossing her head back, revealing well cared for teeth and a strong neckline.

"Yes, even the green ones."

"Well, it was my pleasure, Mrs. Windham. Barry's a fine lad."

"Please," she said, "call me Jean."

"All right, Jean."

"Would—would you like to come in for a cup of coffee, Mr. Pike?"

"Just Pike," he said, "and I'd like that very much. I haven't had a good cup of coffee in a long time."

"I happen to make a very fine cup of coffee, and I'm sure Barry would be thrilled if you . . . um, if you visited."

"I'd like to visit, very much."

She turned to walk back to the house, then looked back over her shoulder to make sure he was following.

Barry Windham was more than thrilled with Pike's presence in his home, and listened avidly as Pike told him stories of traveling through the mountains. Jean Windham also found herself listening fairly intently.

Soon, though, it was time to send Barry to bed.

43

"Aw, Mom—"

"Off you go, Barry," Pike said. "Don't argue with your mother, now. Remember she was right about the vegetables?"

"Yes sir," Barry said, glumly.

"Well, getting the right amount of rest is almost as important."

"Yes sir."

"Come here," Jean said to him, and gathered him in for a kiss goodnight.

"Aw, Ma—" the boy said, embarrassed.

"Good night, Barry."

"Good night, sir—"

"Call me Pike, Barry. Get yourself a good night's sleep."

"'night, Pike."

Barry went off to bed and Jean offered Pike another cup of coffee and another piece of blackberry pie.

"Two pieces is enough, Jean," Pike said, "but I will take one more cup of coffee before I go. It's getting pretty late."

Her invitation for a cup of coffee had extended itself into a two-hour visit, and it was already dark out. She poured him another cup of coffee, which finished the pot.

"I'm glad you stopped me from walking by," Pike told Jean. "To tell you the truth, I've been thinking about you and Barry since I saw you earlier in the evening."

"Really? Why is that?"

"Oh, I guess I get to thinking every so often what it would have been like if I had a family," he said.

"We had a family, for a while," she said, "but now it's just the two of us."

"I understand your husband was killed by a wolf."

"That's right."

44

"And Barry saw it?"

She lowered her eyes and said, "Yes."

"Would you rather not talk about it?"

"No," Jean said, "it's all right. I probably should have talked about it a lot more over the years."

"Maybe with Barry?"

She looked at him and he saw the sadness in her eyes.

"Losing my husband should have been the worse part of it," she said, "but Barry had to see it. He had to watch his father be killed by a pack of wolves."

"I thought Barry said it was one wolf," Pike said, "a one-eyed wolf."

"That's what he said, but no one else has ever seen that one-eyed wolf."

"I have."

"What?"

He told her about the camp being charged by wolves, led by the one-eyed one.

"You actually saw him?"

"Yes," Pike said, "my partner and I both saw him . . . and he saw us."

Jean put her hand to her chest, then to her head.

"Maybe I should have believed Barry a long time ago, but he was so young, and so scared . . ."

"Nobody can blame you for wanting to shelter your son, Jean, but he's what—twelve years old?"

"He'll be thirteen in two months."

"He's a young man," Pike said.

"Yes," Jean Windham said, as if the thought had never occurred to her until, "he is, isn't he?"

Jean walked outside with Pike when he announced it was time for him to leave.

"I have to thank you again," she said, as he stepped down from the porch.

45

"For the vegetables?"

"For a lot more than that, Pike," she said. "Will you be around for a while?"

"For a while."

"Will you come back . . . to see Barry, I mean?"

He smiled at her and said, "I'll come back, Jean, and not just to see Barry—if that's all right with you."

"That's fine with me," she said, "just fine."

"Good night, then."

"Good night, Pike."

When Pike reached his tent he heard sounds coming from McConnell's. He went over quietly and peered inside. McConnell was on his back and there was a woman on top of him. There was enough room in the tent for the woman to be sitting—or rather, bouncing up and down on him. Pike took a moment to watch her breasts bounce tantalizingly, and then cleared his throat.

She caught her breath and looked up at him. He recognized her as Mathilda, the whore from Miss Rachel's.

"Who the hell—" McConnell snapped, looking at Pike upside down.

"It's me, Skins."

"What the hell are you doing here?"

"I heard moans, and thought someone was being killed," Pike said.

"Not yet," Mathilda said, smiling now. She seemed very comfortable, seated astride McConnell like that, and had both of her hands pressed to his chest for support, "but soon."

"If you'll leave us alone."

"I'll leave you alone."

"Wait!"

"What?"

46

Pike stuck his head back into the tent. He could smell Mathilda's sharp, pungent odor and felt himself reacting to it. McConnell looked at him upside down again.

"Where have you been?"

"What do you mean?"

"I thought you said you were coming back here. When I got here, you weren't here."

"Don't tell me you were worried."

"Well, not worried. Maybe just curious."

"I was on my way back here, and I got sidetracked for a while."

"Sidetracked? By what? Or who?"

"Just someone I met."

"A woman?" Mathilda asked.

Pike looked at her and asked, "Are you comfortable?"

"Oh, yes," she said, wiggling her hips.

"Jesus . . ." McConnell said.

"Skins, we can talk about this another time."

"Was it a woman?"

"Later . . ." Pike said, and withdrew from the tent.

"'bye," he heard Mathilda say.

Pike walked back to his tent and crawled inside. It was dark, and it smelled. It was a damp, cloying smell, like the wet fur of an animal. He reached around for the oil lamp and fished into his pocket for a match. While he was doing this his eyes began to adjust to the darkness. Also, he suddenly felt as if he wasn't alone.

Then, from the other side of the tent—which was only about ten feet long—he saw something. A shape, or the outline of a shape, and then the glint of something—like an eye.

Like a single eye.

That was when Ol' One-Eye growled, and Pike froze with the match in his hand.

Chapter Five

For the first time in his life Jack Pike did not know what to do. He considered soiling his pants, but that wouldn't have accomplished anything. Sweat was starting to roll down his face, and he could feel it rolling down to the small of his back, as well.

On the other hand, the wolf seemed similarly at a loss as to what to do next. It would have been very easy for the animal to spring at him and tear out his throat. Why didn't it?

Pike knew his rifle and Kentucky pistol were in the tent somewhere, but he couldn't quite remember where, at the moment. He had his knife at his side, but his right hand was still elevated, holding the match.

The match.

Any animal, no matter what his legend was, disliked fire, didn't it?

It was time to find out.

Using his thumbnail Pike scraped the match, and it flared to life. By the glow of it he could see Ol' One-Eye's one eye squint against the light. The animal might even have shrunk back from the fire a bit.

The entire tent seemed to be filled with the huge wolf, and Pike could feel the animal's hot breath on his face.

Still, the animal didn't move, and it seemed entranced by the flame.

Pike knew he didn't have long before the match burned down. His original intention had been to back out of the tent, holding the flame between him and One-Eye. Now, however, he could see his rifle and it was within reach. If he did reach for it, though, what would the wolf do?

Pike decided he'd better get out into the open before the match went out.

Slowly, he started to back out, and still the wolf didn't move. He was almost out of the tent completely when a breeze blew the match out, throwing the tent into total darkness.

But he was outside.

"Jesus," he said to himself. The breeze seemed like ice on his sweating face. He watched the entrance of the tent intently, but the wolf didn't seem to be ready to leave.

Keeping his eye on the tent he backed his way to McConnell's tent.

"Skins," he said, in a low voice.

From inside he could hear harsh breathing, sighs and moans.

"Skins," he said, louder.

"What now," McConnell's muffled voice asked from inside his tent.

"Your rifle."

"What?"

"I need your rifle!"

"What for?"

"The wolf—"

"What?"

"The goddamned one-eyed wolf is in my tent!" he said urgently.

50

"Jesus," McConnell said. Suddenly, his head appeared from inside the tent. "Really?"

"I crawled into my tent," Pike said, "and there he was."

"Christ!"

"I need your rifle."

"He's still in there?"

"Yes!"

McConnell moved, and the butt of his rifle appeared.

"Let me get dressed."

"No time," Pike said, taking the rifle.

"Pike—" McConnell said as Pike moved away from the tent and back toward his own. "Are you sure he's still in there?"

"I've been watching," Pike said, "and he ain't left yet."

McConnell crawled out of his tent buck naked, dragging his pants with him. He pulled the pants on and followed Pike.

"You gonna fire through the tent or try to flush him out?"

"I don't know," Pike said, cautiously advancing on his tent, McConnell close behind him.

"I wonder where his pack is?"

"Well, they weren't in the tent with him and me," Pike said. "I would have noticed."

When they reached the tent they stopped, Pike pointing the rifle at the tent entrance.

"Maybe I should get some help," McConnell said.

"No time," Pike said. "I'm going in."

"Back inside?"

"I've got this now," Pike said, indicating the rifle.

"Well, just stick the barrel in and fire."

"No," Pike said, "I want to see him."

51

"Pike—"

"Stand clear, Skins," Pike said. As an afterthought he took his knife from his belt and said, "Here," handing it to McConnell.

"Good luck," McConnell said.

Pike crouched down and used the barrel of the rifle to move the tent flap aside. Slowly, he moved forward, peering inside the tent. Holding the rifle in one hand, he took out another match and used his nail to bring it to life.

By the light of the match he could see that the tent was empty.

How could that be?

He entered the tent and looked around, but he was being ridiculous now. There was nowhere in the small tent that a wolf could hide . . . but he had watched the entrance to the tent the whole time, and the wolf had not come out.

"Pike?" McConnell called.

Pike didn't answer.

"Hey, Pike, are you all right?"

Pike crawled to the end of the tent to check the rear, but there were no holes, no slits in the fabric. He could still smell the wolf, though, so he knew he hadn't dreamt it. The animal had been there!

"Pike, damn it, answer me!"

"I'm coming out."

He backed out of the tent and stood up.

"Well?" McConnell asked.

"He's not in there."

"He got away?"

"He can't have," Pike said. "I was watching the tent the whole time. He couldn't have gotten out."

"If he was in there in the first place," McConnell said.

Pike looked at McConnell and said, "You think I made it up?"

"I didn't say that."

"Then what? I dreamt it?"

"Pike—"

"Dann it, Skins, the damned wolf was in there! Go inside, you can still smell him."

"Then where is he now, Pike?"

"I don't know."

Both of them started looking around them, as if they expected Ol' One-Eye and his whole pack to come tearing down on them.

"Well," McConnell finally said, "I guess he's gone now." He reached over and took his rifle from Pike's hands. "Let's get some sleep."

"Sleep," Pike said, as if that were the farthest thing from his mind.

"Go on, Pike," McConnell said. "We'll try and figure it out in the morning."

McConnell went back to his own tent while Pike stood outside his staring at it. He knew that if he went inside and tried to sleep he'd only be able to smell that damned wolf.

He had to find someplace else to sleep.

Pike took his rifle from the tent and walked back to the settlement. He found Miss Rachel's and entered.

"Kind of late, ain't it?" Miss Rachel asked.

"I need a bed."

"And a girl?"

"Just a place to sleep."

"This ain't a hotel," the woman said. "You want a bed, you get a girl with it. Same price."

"All right, I'll take a girl."

"Blonde, brunette or redhead?"

Pike was about to answer that he'd leave it up to her

53

when something occurred to him.

"I want Maria."

"Sorry," Miss Rachel said, "but she's not one of the girls."

"She's a girl, ain't she?"

"Yes, but—"

"I want her," Pike said, "Maria and a bed." He took some money out of his pocket. "Is this enough?"

She took the money he offered, folded it and shoved it down the front of her wrap without showing him what was inside.

"I'll send her right out."

She went off and moments later Maria came walking up to him.

"Follow me," she said.

He followed her past the partition where he'd bathed to another, where there was a bed. He idly wondered how many whores had come from the east carrying mattresses with them. The whorehouse tent at Clark's Fork was also filled with real mattresses.

"There is your bed," Maria said. "Do you want me to undress?"

"No," Pike said, sitting on the bed. "Maria, all I want is some sleep. You can sleep beside me, dressed or naked, that's up to you. Or you can sleep on the floor. I promise I won't touch you."

"I knew it," she said. "You're like the others."

"What others?"

"The other men who don't want me because of this," she said, pointing to the scar on her face.

"Maria, any man who would turn you away because of that is a fool."

"What about you?"

"I'm just too damned tired to do anything but sleep," he said. "I promise you, the scar has nothing to do with it."

"Sure," she said, glumly. "For a moment, when Miss Rachel said you asked for me, I thought—"

"Jesus," Pike said, closing his eyes. He didn't have time for this. "Maria, just go to sleep. I'll make it up to you another time. I promise."

"You promise . . ." Maria said.

Pike pulled off his boots, removed his shirt and trousers, laid the rifle next to the bed and lay down on his back.

"Do whatever you want," he said to the girl, "but I'm going to sleep."

He lay there with his eyes closed for a little while, drifting off, and then felt the mattress give under her slight weight. She moved around a bit next to him, and then settled down with her hips against his. He could feel the heat of her right through his longjohns.

The little bitch had gotten into bed naked.

Pike did his best to ignore the fact that Maria was lying next to him naked, and finally was able to fall asleep. He awakened sometime later, though, to find her sitting astride him. Through his longjohns he could feel the intense heat of her pussy.

"Maria—"

"I just want to show you," she said, "that I'm as good as any of them."

"I believe you, honey," he said, reaching for her shoulders. She moved, however, and his hands came into contact with her small, but hard breasts. He squeezed and was impressed. It was like squeezing two not quite ripe peaches. When he touched her nipples with his thumbs she closed her eyes and moaned.

"Jesus," he said, and started to unbutton his longjohns. Maria hopped off him and helped him out of the long underwear. By this time his penis was erect and rock hard, a condition which did not escape her notice.

"Watch," she said, and brought her mouth down on him. He didn't watch so much as "feel," as she began to ride him up and down with her mouth. He became convinced that, at one time or another, she was a whore and that the scar had driven her from the profession. He thought that was a shame, because she was extremely good at what she was doing.

When he thought he was going to explode into her mouth she released him and grinned at him.

"Did you ever have it better?" she demanded. "Huh?"

"Maria—" he said, weakly.

She hopped astride him then and began to rub her furry patch up and down the length of him. He finally decided to take charge. He grabbed her by the hips, raised her up and brought her down on him hard, impaling her. She gasped, her eyes widening, and reached out, bracing her hands against his chest. Still holding her by the hips he began to ride her up and down on his cock. She weighed almost nothing, but her pussy was both hot and tight, and soon he was moving his own hips, as well. When he released her she just kept on bouncing up and down on him, and when she finally brought herself down hard and stayed there, swiveling on him while she came, he released himself and exploded inside of her . . .

This time when he drifted off to sleep it was with Maria lying in the crook of his arm. He was able to reach her breasts with his hand, and held one while they slept . . .

When morning came he woke to find her head down

between his legs, her tongue artfully teasing him erect.

"Maria—"

"This time," she said, "you just lie still, and I'll do all the work."

True to her word her talented mouth swooped down on him and she sucked him, fondling his balls, until he finally gave her what she wanted, groaning and lifting his hips as he ejaculated . . .

As he dressed in the morning she watched him from the bed.

"There's something I don't understand," he said to her.

"What?"

"In the bath you begged me not to touch you."

"I know," she said, "but I really wanted you to."

"Then why—"

"I haven't been with a man, Pike, in two years, since a man did this to me with a knife, rather than pay me," she said, pointing to the scar. "I've hated men ever since then. It was a man who did this to me, and ever since then men haven't looked at me the same. They haven't wanted me."

"They were fools."

"I realize that now, and I realize now that it was foolish to hate all men for what some men did. All I needed was to find a man like you."

"Don't make me out to be something special, Maria," Pike said. "There are plenty of other men who will look past the scar, if you give them the chance."

"I'm going to talk to Miss Rachel," Maria said, "and see if she'll give me the chance."

"I'll talk to her on the way out," Pike said.

"No, don't." She came to her knees on the bed and grabbed his arm.

"Why not?"

"Because I don't want you to pay for what we had last night. All right?"

He smiled and said, "All right."

"Will you come back?" she asked.

He leaned over and kissed her and said, "I'll come back."

As he left he felt that he owed it to her to come back. After all, thanks to her he hadn't thought about that damned one-eyed wolf all night.

Chapter Six

Pike met up with McConnell in front of the trading post. Pike had been on his way to wake his friend up.

"Where'd you spend the night?" McConnell asked. "I checked your tent."

"I couldn't get rid of the wolf smell, so I went to Miss Rachel's."

"Ah," McConnell said, "found an entirely different smell there, I'll bet."

"I got some sleep," Pike said, "and that's what I was after."

"And did you get something else you weren't after?" McConnell asked with raised eyebrows.

"Are you interested in breakfast?"

"How could I not be?" McConnell asked. "Most everyone else in our little tent community is out in front of their tent cooking. The smells woke me up."

"What about Mathilda?"

"Yeah," McConnell said, grinning, "those smells woke me up, too."

Pike shook his head and said, "Let's go inside and see if we can get some breakfast from Locke."

When they got inside they got more than breakfast from Locke. They got the news that some animals had been brought down by wolves during the night.

"Well," Pike said, "I wasn't sure I was going to mention it, but I had my own little run-in with a wolf last night."

"What wolf?" Locke asked. He had brought them each a cup of coffee.

"A one-eyed wolf."

"Let me bring you gents some eggs, and then we can talk about it."

"Fine," Pike said.

As Locke went away McConnell said, "Two mules and a horse. This pack seems to have an appetite for one kind of meat."

"Let's hope they don't graduate to human meat," Pike said.

They worked on their coffee until Locke returned with two plates of bacon and eggs, some biscuits, and a pot of coffee. He laid it all down on the table and then sat down with them. At the same time he waved to another man, who came over.

The newcomer was about five foot eight, but he was easily as wide as Pike. He had about a week's worth of beard growth, and smelled like he hadn't been near water for an equal amount of time. Pike could afford to make comments like that to himself because he'd had a bath yesterday.

"Pike, McConnell, this is De Roche."

"Pleased," De Roche said.

"De Roche hunts wolves," Locke said. "Would you mind if he heard what happened last night?"

"No, I don't mind," Pike said. "Pull up a seat, De Roche."

De Roche nodded and sat and Pike told them what had happened in his tent last night.

"Merde," De Roche said, "ze animal sounds like a demon."

"Not a demon," Pike said, "just a crafty wolf."

"Ha," De Roche said, "around here, ze Snake and Nez Perce think he is a demon."

"We're a little smarter than that, though, aren't we, De Roche?" Pike asked.

"Are we?" De Roche asked.

"Have you had any dealings with Ol' One-Eye before?" McConnell asked.

"I have hunted many wolves," De Roche said, "but not this one—not yet."

"I've asked De Roche to hunt Ol' One-Eye down and kill him," Locke said. "I was sort of hoping you boys would go along. We're payin' good money for that devil's hide."

"We're trappers," Pike said, "not hunters—not for hire, anyway. And I wouldn't be calling that wolf a devil, you're liable to spook some people."

"The people around here are already spooked," Locke said. "That pack came into the settlement in the dead of night, and you're the only one who saw anything. Besides, I'd think you'd be spooked after what you went through last night."

"Not spooked enough to start thinking that some wolf is a devil, or a demon, and not enough to start hunting him for money. Sorry, Locke. I'm speaking for myself, though. Skins?"

Locke looked hopefully at McConnell.

"I feel the same way, Locke," McConnell said. "Sorry."

"Zere is no problem," De Roche said, standing. "I have my men, and we will catch this de—this wolf."

"I wish you luck," Pike said.

"I appreciate zat, but I do not need luck. I am the finest hunter in the mountains." De Roche looked at Locke and said, "We must conclude the first half of our business arrangement."

61

"I've got the money," Locke said. "I'll get it."

De Roche went back to his own table without further word to Pike or McConnell. As Locke stood up Pike grabbed his forearm.

"You paying him in advance?"

"Half," Locke said, "half in advance, the other half when he brings in the hide."

"You better make sure he brings you the head intact," Pike said, "so you can check the one eye."

Locke's eyes widened and he said, "Good point, Pike. Thanks."

"Sure."

"You know, I've heard of you before, Pike. I sure wish you were goin' with him."

"Sorry."

Locke nodded and went to get De Roche the first half of his money, money which had probably been collected from the other people at the settlement.

"What do you think of De Roche?" McConnell asked.

"Didn't see enough to form an opinion," Pike said. "You ever heard of him before?"

"No."

"Me neither," Pike said. "That bothers me . . . I mean, if he's really the best hunter in the mountains."

"I'll bet there are some folks hereabouts who haven't heard of you, either."

"Probably," Pike said, "but then I don't go around claiming to be the best at anything."

"You don't have to," McConnell pointed out.

"I'm going to eat these eggs before they get cold," Pike said, then took a bite and added, "or colder."

Jean Windham was worried. Already she had heard from two of her neighbors about the wolf pack that had

62

come into the settlement and taken the lives of some animals. At least no people had been hurt, but she was now leery of letting Barry out that day.

"I'm gonna do my chores, Ma," Barry said, heading for the door.

"What's your hurry?" she asked. "Want some more flapjacks?"

"I already had two stacks, Ma," Barry said, grinning. "Whataya wanna do, make me fat?"

"I've just never seen you in a hurry to do chores before," she said. "I'm amazed."

Her son turned his back to the door and stared at her.

"Maybe you're just worried about them wolves."

She looked fondly at her son and said, "What makes you so smart?"

"I'm growin' up," he said.

"I know," Jean said. "Don't think I haven't noticed that."

"Don't worry, Ma," Barry said, "I'll be careful."

"I know you will."

He turned and went out the door, and she shook her head at how fast her son was growing up.

Outside Barry Windham went about his chores, trying to finish them as fast as he could. What his mother didn't know was that he had plans of his own for those wolves—that is, for the one-eyed wolf which had killed his father. Barry still had his father's rifle, and he was going to use it to kill that one-eyed wolf, and avenge his father.

If his mother knew that—boy, she *never* would have let him out of the house.

*   *   *

63

Standing outside the trading post, their bellies full, Pike and McConnell were at a loss as to what to do.

They looked at each other and Pike said, "I think I've had enough of this place already."

"I know what you mean," McConnell said. "Time to be moving on."

"Stock, or supplies?" Pike asked.

"I'll go back inside and stock up," McConnell said. "Why don't you go and get us a horse and another mule? I trust your judgment."

"Thanks," Pike said. "Make sure you don't forget the coffee."

"I won't forget the coffee," McConnell said. "When did I ever forget the coffee?"

"There was that time in Clark's Fork, when Clark had that girl working his counter—"

"Never mind," McConnell said. "I won't forget this time."

Pike went first to talk to Franks, the man who had rented them the tents and cared for their horse. He was a tall, white-haired man with an accent Pike couldn't place. Pike had never met a man from England before. Forty-five years old, Franks had come to this country twenty years earlier. It took him six years to find the Rockies, and when he did he fell in love with them. The accent, however, remained intact, except got an occasional lapse into "I gots" and "I reckons" that he had picked up after so many years in the west.

"I can sell you a horse, that's no problem," Franks said, rubbing his swollen belly absently, "but I don't have any mules. I can tell you who does, though."

"Who?"

"A Frenchman named De Roche."

"De Roche."

64

Franks frowned and said, "Do you know him?"

"Met him this morning, as a matter of fact."

"Well, he's got more mules than he needs. You might talk to him about buying one."

"I'll do that," Pike said. "What kind of shape is the horse we brought in yesterday in?"

"He's a good animal. He's in fine shape."

"Got one like him?"

Franks grinned and said, "Come with me and I'll show you what I've got."

Pike and Franks dickered for a while before coming to terms on a price for a sure-footed, four-year-old, mountain raised colt. Pike told Franks that they would need both animals to be ready at first light.

"They'll be ready," Franks said. "I heard that you had a visitor last night."

"An uninvited one."

"That would have scared the hell out of me," Franks said.

"What makes you think it didn't scare the hell out of me?"

"I've heard of you, Pike," Franks said. "You can't live in these mountains as long as I have and not hear the stories, and the legends."

"Which am I," Pike asked, "story or legend."

"You're a legend with a story," Franks said. "Are you going to hunt the one-eyed wolf?"

"What makes you ask that?"

"Just something I heard."

"I don't know what you heard," Pike said, "but I'm leaving tomorrow—providing I can get a mule, that is."

"De Roche will sell you a mule," Franks said with certainty, "but he's a hard trader."

"Tell me about De Roche?"

"What's to tell?" Franks said. "I'm from England, he's from France, we've both been in the mountains about the same amount of time, we both still have some of our accent. He's a hunter, mostly, and I'm a trader . . . mostly. We're a lot alike, actually."

"Not from what I've seen, so far," Pike said.

"De Roche is a little harder, a little more cynical than I am," Franks said, "and he might not be quite as honest as I am."

"I'll keep that in mind," Pike said. "See you in the morning."

"Your animals will be ready," Franks said. "In fact, when you get your mule bring it to me and I'll see that it's packed and ready, too."

"Appreciate it," Pike said, and went in search of De Roche.

As he went looking for De Roche he kept Franks' words in mind. He hadn't liked the Frenchman on first meeting, and he didn't think that trading with him was going to change his opinion.

Asking around, he finally found De Roche's camp, but no one was there. There was a large tent, and a smaller one, and some animals tethered together. There were about a half a dozen mules and Pike started to walk over to examine them when he spotted something that made him stop. He walked over to a stack of skins and examined them closely, something starting to take shape in the pit of his stomach.

The skins looked like the ones he and McConnell had lost to the wolves in their camp several nights earlier. They had wondered what a pack of wolves would want with skins, and maybe he had found the answer.

Chapter Seven

"Can I do something for you?"

Pike turned at the sound of De Roche's voice behind him. He stood almost a foot taller than the Frenchman, but standing there looking at the other man, he knew that he would be a formidable opponent.

"Nice skins," he said.

"Thank you."

"I thought you were a hunter, not a trapper."

De Roche shrugged, his eyes fixed on Pike.

"You do what you have to do to survive."

"You intend to sell these to Locke?"

"Maybe," De Roche said. "Is there something I can do for you, Pike?"

"Yeah, fella named Franks says you might be able to sell me a mule."

"I might," De Roche said. "Did you lose yours?"

"To the wolves."

"That is unfortunate."

"Yeah," Pike said, "we thought so, too."

The two men stood there studying each other for a few moments, and then De Roche broke the tableau.

"Come," he said, "pick one out and we will discuss price."

Pike came away from his meeting with De Roche convinced of two things. One, he was as tough a trader as Franks had said he would be, and two, the stack of skins were the ones Pike and McConnell had collected. Somehow, De Roche had ended up with them. Pike would have liked to know how, but that would mean staying around Fort Hall longer than he intended. It might even mean going hunting with De Roche, and he didn't want to do that.

"When are you leaving for the hunt?" Pike asked before leaving De Roche's camp.

"This evening."

"Evening?" Pike said, frowning. "You're not waiting until morning?"

De Roche shook his head, but did not explain his reasoning.

"Well, suit yourself," Pike said. "Thanks for the mule."

"You paid for it."

"Thanks, anyway," Pike said, and left the camp, leading the animal.

He took the mule and turned it over to Franks.

"Get a decent price?" Franks asked.

"No."

"I told you he was mean."

"He knew I needed it," Pike said, "and took advantage of it."

"That's what I said," Franks said, "mean."

Pike left Franks and went looking for McConnell.

"Are you sure they were our skins?"

"How can I be sure?" Pike asked. "We didn't brand the damned things . . . but I'm almost sure."

They were seated by a fire they had set in front of

McConnell's tent. Around them were other fires, and other men. They had exchanged nods with some of the other men, but formal introductions had not been made.

"How did he get the damned things?"

"I don't know," Pike said, "and that's the point. Do we want to forget it, or do we want to stay around here and find out."

McConnell made a face.

"Staying around here doesn't appeal to me."

"What about Mathilda?"

"There are other Mathildas."

Pike rubbed the back of his neck.

"He could have come across the camp and figured it was deserted," he reasoned. "It certainly wouldn't have taken a genius to see what had happened."

"Yeah, but he heard what happened to us," McConnell said. "He's got to know that camp was ours, and the skins are ours. If he was an honest man he'd turn them over to us."

"He might be waiting for us to lay claim."

"Sure."

"Did you talk to Locke about him?"

"Yeah," McConnell said. "This is a dangerous man, Pike. I mean, he ain't very big, but he's mean and he's dangerous. Locke even suggested he might be a little crazy."

"Or more than a little."

"Let's sleep on it," McConnell said. "We're ready to go in the morning, but we can always change our minds."

"All right," Pike said, "all right, we'll sleep on it."

"Okay," McConnell said, "but what do we do with the rest of the day?"

"Well, I know what I'm going to do," Pike said, standing up.

"What?"

"I'm going to visit a boy and his mother."

"You like that boy, huh?"

"Yeah," Pike said, "I guess I do."

Jean Windham was worried.

She hadn't seen Barry since he'd finished his chores and had lunch, and only moments ago she had noticed that her husband's old rifle was gone.

Please God, she prayed, let him be hunting rabbits.

McConnell remained seated in front of his tent after Pike left, and minutes later a man approached him.

"'scuse me," the man said, "but I couldn't help overhearing your conversation."

"That so?" McConnell asked, looking up at the man. He was slightly built, probably De Roche's height but a good fifty to sixty pounds lighter.

"The name's Tolan," the man said, "and I've had some dealings with De Roche."

"So?"

"I was figgerin' maybe it might be worth somethin' to you to have us talk about him a spell."

McConnell eyed the man with distaste now. Obviously the man had been eavesdropping, and thought he saw a way to make some easy money.

The man started to sit opposite McConnell.

"Don't sit down," McConnell said. "I didn't invite you to sit."

"Whataya say?" Tolan said. "We got a deal?"

"I don't think so."

"It pays to know your enemy," Tolan said, rubbing his hand together.

"Right now I don't figure I got any enemies."

"De Roche is a bad man—"

"Look," McConnell said, cutting the man off, "I

ain't payin' you any money, so get lost."

"Don't got to be so rough," the man said, pouting. "I was just trying to help."

"I know what you were tryin' to do," McConnell said, "so go and try it somewhere else."

The man backed away, muttering to himself, then turned and hurried off.

McConnell wondered if he was going to offer De Roche the same deal.

Barry Windham was scared, only he didn't want to admit it. He was holding his father's rifle so tightly that his hands were starting to sweat.

Already he had wandered farther away from his house than he had in the past, but he figured that was what he had to do to find that one-eyed wolf. With his father dead he hadn't had a man to teach him hunting while he grew up, so he wasn't taking the proper precautions. His movements were too noisy, and he wasn't at all sure what he was looking and listening for.

He was out of his element, but all he could think of was his father being brought down by the weight of that one-eyed wolf. The vision if it was still clear in his head. Every time he dreamt of it, his father's blood seemed a brighter red.

He wanted to see if that wolf's blood was the same color.

When Pike knocked on Jean Windham's door he was surprised when it was opened so abruptly.

"Oh, Pike," she said, and then hopefully, "have you seen Barry?"

"No," Pike said, "I was coming to see him now. He's not here?"

"He's gone," she said, wiping her hands on an apron

she was wearing. "He left just after lunch, after he finished his chores."

"Well, he must have friends," Pike said. "Maybe he went to play with them."

"His father's rifle is gone."

"Oh? Does he hunt?"

"Rabbits," she said, a faraway look in her eyes, "that's all he's ever hunted, rabbits."

"Jean," Pike said, taking her by the shoulders, "where do you think he's gone."

"God help him," she said, "I think he's gone after that wolf."

"What does he know about the wolf?"

"We heard, this morning, about the wolves, about the one-eyed wolf—my God, Pike, I can't lose him, too. I can't." She gripped his forearms so hard that her nails dug into him.

"Just relax," he said. "Stay here, Jean, and wait, in case he comes back."

"What are you going to do?"

"I'll get Skins and we'll look for him," Pike said, "we'll find him, I promise."

"If anything happens to him . . ."

"We'll find him," Pike said, again, "just stay here and wait."

As he rushed away from the house he couldn't help thinking that in telling her to wait he had given her the hardest job.

When Pike reached McConnell they exchanged stories, McConnell's about a man named Tolan, and Pike's about Barry Windham.

"You figure Tolan went to De Roche after you?" Pike asked.

"I would if I was a coyote like him," McConnell said. "Tryin' to get paid by both sides."

"Well, I can't deal with that now," Pike said. "We've got to find that boy, Skins, before he finds that wolf . . . or the other way around."

"I'll get my rifle and we'll go," McConnell said. "You want to split up?"

Pike nodded.

"We'll cover more ground that way."

"Then get goin'," McConnell said. "I'll take north, and then east."

"Fine."

"When do we meet?"

"Skins," Pike said, "we keep looking until we find him."

Ol' One-Eye watched the small human stumble his way through the woods. There was not enough there to make a meal of, if One-Eye was even interested in human food—which he wasn't. Still, the old wolf followed the small human because there was something very familiar about him.

Chapter Eight

Pike chastized himself while he searched for Barry Windham. He'd had two chances to kill that one-eyed wolf, once in their camp, and once in his own damned tent, and he hadn't done so either time. If that wolf killed young Barry, the way he had killed the boy's father, Pike would never forgive himself.

He had to find that boy.

Waiting was killing Jean, and she finally decided that she would wait no longer. She changed into trousers and a shirt, pulled on a pair of boots, and left the house to look for her boy herself.

McConnell scanned the woods for that shock of white-blond hair that topped the boy's head. Spotting the boy should be very easy. The hard part, however, might be in finding him before he found the wolf—and before the one-eyed wolf, or the whole damned pack, found him.

*   *   *

Barry started to sense that he was in trouble. He was pretty far from his house now, and it was coming on evening. If he didn't find that wolf pretty quick he could get stuck out here in the dark, and he had never had anyone to teach him how to survive in the woods, in the dark.

He turned to go back, and then realized that he wasn't really sure which way was back.

Now he was scared.

Ol' One-Eye sensed the confusion in the small human, and he smelled the fear. Suddenly, the small human became quarry—confused, frightened quarry. He was standing still, and the wolf was circling him, looking for the best angle to charge from.

There was still something very familiar about this small human, something that made Ol' One-Eye think that it was time to close in.

Damn, Pike was thinking, damn, damn, where the hell had the boy gotten to.

"Barry!"

It had only been the last few minutes that he had taken to calling out to the boy.

"Barry! Where are you?"

He hoped that the boy would hear him and respond. Hopefully, the boy wouldn't *not* respond, thinking that he had to avoid being found until he could find the wolf. He must know by now that his mother would have someone looking for him.

Pike was starting to feel panic. It was obvious that the wolves were still in the area. Barry had heard about his encounter with Ol' One-Eye, and had seen it as a chance to get revenge on the animal for killing his father. The headstrong boy had not thought about his own safety, but as darkness came, he would *start* to think about it.

Hopefully, the boy would be so scared that he'd start back—if he knew the way back.

Barry thought he heard something, a rustling sound. The woods were the thickest here, and he stood in a clearing and tried to stare into them to see what was making the noise. He held the rifle up and ready, and tried to push away the fear and stay alert. Barry Windham was running on instinct, now, gripping the rifle tightly and waiting.

Jean Windham felt that her son was helpless out there. Without a father to teach him the things he should know, how could he go hunting for a wolf and have even a small chance of finding it and killing it? If he even happened upon the wolf, the animal would kill him, the way it had killed his father.

Jean had no weapon, but if she came across her son and the wolf, without hesitation she would throw herself between them.

Ol' One-Eye found the angle he wanted, and started to close on the boy.

Pike found the tracks he was looking for, and the tracks he didn't want to find. In the dirt he saw the small tracks of a twelve-year-old boy, and he saw the large paw prints that could only belong to Ol' One-Eye. Some of the wolf's tracks were made right over the boy's, which meant that the wolf was stalking the boy.

Pike quickened his pace and followed the tracks, hoping he would get there in time.

Suddenly, the boy knew the wolf was there, behind him. It was as if he could feel the animal's hot breath on the back of his neck. Barry tightened his hands on the rifle, turned and found himself looking into the single eye of a wolf.

Barry had seen wolves before—in fact, he had seen *this* wolf before—but he didn't think he had ever seen a wolf this big. The single eye was fixed on him, and the animal's tongue was hanging out, dripping saliva.

"You killed my father," Barry said to the beast. "Now I'm gonna kill you."

He started to raise the rifle, and the wolf sprang.

Pike heard the screams, and the growls, and broke into a run. He ran as hard as his long legs would take him, and the sounds of the struggle came closer and closer. When he reached the clearing he couldn't believe what he was seeing.

Twelve-year-old Barry Windham was bloody, but he was on his feet, holding his father's rifle crossways. Hanging onto the rifle was Ol' One-Eye, his powerful jaws clamped down onto the barrel.

Linked together by the rifle, they were going around and around, and Pike was trying to draw a bead on the animal.

"Damn," he said, as the duo continued their dance. Abruptly, he discarded the rifle, drew his knife and charged them.

As he closed on them, the wolf abruptly released the rifle and turned to face Pike. Barry, no longer locked

78

together with the wolf, simply kneeled over and fell to the ground. The wolf moved closer to the fallen boy, as if he was protecting him rather than menacing him.

Pike stopped, and faced the wolf. If he charged the animal the wolf would still have time to clamp his jaws down on the boy's neck and snap it. Suddenly, Pike was sorry he had discarded his rifle, but he still had his Kentucky pistol in his belt. Slowly, he put the knife away and produced the pistol. At that point, someone else entered the clearing, and screamed.

"Barry!"

Somehow, without knowing where she was going, Jean Windham had stumbled upon the tableau as it existed at that point. The boy was on the ground, covered with blood; the wolf, standing right next to the boy; Pike, facing the wolf with a pistol in his hand.

At the sound of her scream both Pike and the wolf looked her way.

"Jean!" Pike shouted. "Get out of here."

Instead of doing that, however, Jean Windham ran directly toward her son—and the wolf.

Pike watched in amazement as the woman seemed to charge the wolf . . . and the wolf turned and ran!

Jean Windham reached her son and kneeled by his side, taking him in her arms. Pike, still leery about the wolf possibly coming back, knelt next to her, the pistol still in his hand.

"Barry," Jean cried, "oh Barry . . ."

It took only one look for Pike to determine that the boy was badly mauled, but he was alive.

"We've got to get him back, Jean," Pike said. "Give him to me."

He handed her the pistol and scooped the boy up in his arms. His limp form was almost weightless in his powerful arms.

"Just watch out for the wolf, or the pack," he told her. "If you see him, don't think and don't hesitate, just fire the pistol."

"I will."

Neither of them wanted to think what would happen if she missed.

"Pick up my rifle and let's go."

"Will he be all right?" she asked, anxiously, running to keep up with him.

"He's alive," Pike said, "but we've got to get him back to the settlement as fast as we can. We've got to run, Jean. Can you keep up?"

"God help him," she said, "let's run—and don't wait for me."

They ran.

Ol' One-Eye watched from a distance as the two adult humans ran, carrying the smaller human. The wolf licked his muzzle, still tasting the blood of the small human—a taste he found very familiar to him. It was a taste he wanted to sample again.

But the animal had felt something from the female human that he had never felt before. In the face of her charge, he had turned and run. That disturbed him, so for now he simply followed them.

Chapter Nine

Skins McConnell was waiting for Pike when the big man came out of the doctor's tent.

"How's the kid?" McConnell asked.

"I don't know yet," Pike said. "He's pretty well torn up."

"Torn up? That what the doctor says?"

"Doctor." Pike snorted. "They don't have a doctor. They got the same guy working on the kid that works on their animals."

"No doctor?"

"They never had one."

"That poor kid . . ."

"Yeah," Pike said, "and his mother."

"How is she?"

"How would you be if he was your kid?"

McConnell just shook his head, then noticed that Pike was looking off into the distance.

"Uh-oh."

Pike looked at McConnell.

"What do you mean, uh-oh?"

"The way you look."

"What's the matter with the way I look?"

"What are you thinkin' about?"

"Skins—"

"No, no, Jack," McConnell said, "I know you. You got somethin' on your mind. What is it?"

Pike stared at McConnell for a moment, then said, "I'm going after that wolf, Skins."

"I knew it."

"I'm not asking you to come—"

"You don't have to ask," McConnell said, "you know that. If you're goin', I'm goin'."

"Thanks, Skins."

"The kid mean that much to you, Pike?"

"I like him, Skins," Pike said, "and I want that devil wolf."

"Whoa," McConnell said, putting his hand on Pike's shoulders, "let's not let this get out of hand. If we're gonna hunt, we're gonna hunt a wolf, not a devil. All right?"

"Agreed," Pike said, but McConnell wasn't so sure that he did agree. "Let's go and see Locke."

Locke liked the idea of Pike and McConnell going after the wolf, but he saw one problem.

"What problem?" Pike asked.

"De Roche," Locke said. "He's not gonna like the competition—unless you plan on goin' with him."

"No," Pike said, "I won't hunt with De Roche."

"Why not?" Locke asked.

"I don't like him."

Locke shrugged and said, "I guess that's a good enough reason, but what are you going to do about him?"

"Why do I have to do anything about him?" Pike asked. "If he gets the wolf, he gets paid."

"And if you get it," Locke said, "he doesn't."

"Right."

Locke pointed his finger and said, "That's the problem."

Pike stared at Locke for a few moments, then looked at McConnell.

"Maybe we better go and talk to the man," McConnell said.

When they reached De Roche's camp he was still there, but they could tell he was moments away from breaking camp and pulling out. He was putting the finishing touches to a pack mule.

"De Roche."

The Frenchman turned around and frowned when he saw Pike.

"What is wrong?" he asked. "You don't like ze mule? Too bad, I don't take her back. When we make a deal—"

"The mule's fine, De Roche," Pike said.

De Roche looked disappointed that Pike hadn't come to argue over the mule.

"What do you want, then?" he asked. "I am pulling out very soon, and I do not have much time."

"I just wanted to tell you that we're going after that wolf."

De Roche stopped what he was doing and turned around. His glare was mean, and there was a touch of concern there, as well.

"What?"

"I said we're going after the wolf."

De Roche took two steps and then stopped.

"I am being paid to kill that wolf."

"Well, I'm not."

"Oh, yes," the Frenchman said, "you are hunting ze wolf for the sport, yes?"

"No."

"Of course not," De Roche said. "You want my money."

83

"I just want the wolf killed, De Roche. I don't care if you do it, or I do it."

"I care," De Roche said. "If you kill it, I do not get paid." He took several more steps until he was about three feet from Pike. "I tell you this, if you get in my way I will kill you. You understand?"

"I understand, De Roche," Pike said. "I don't want to get in your way, I only want that wolf dead."

"Remember what I say now, Pike," De Roche said. "I don't care who you are, I will not let you take my wolf from me."

"Your wolf?"

"That is right, my wolf. I have been paid half my money, and I will collect the other half."

"Come on, Jack," McConnell said, grabbing Pike's elbow. "Come on. There's no reasoning with him."

"You cannot reason with a thief!" De Roche said.

"Are you calling me a thief?" Pike said.

"Jack, come on—" McConnell said, but Pike shook off his hand.

"De Roche, I'm doing this for a boy who was mauled by that wolf a little while ago, and for the boy's mother. This wolf killed the boy's father, and today he tried to kill the boy. I'm not going to let that happen."

"You are a great and noble man, Jack Pike," De Roche said sarcastically, "but that does not mean that I will not kill you if you try to come between me and my wolf."

"You're crazy, De Roche!" Pike said. "This isn't a competition."

De Roche shook his head and waved a hand at Pike, walking back to his pack mule. When he reached the mule he turned, looked at Pike and said, "It is now."

Pike and McConnell went to break their camps, as

well, and get ready to leave in the morning. Even though De Roche was leaving tonight, for his own reasons, they didn't think it likely he would find the wolf that night.

"You want to find this wolf before De Roche does, don't you?" McConnell asked.

"Yes."

"Why?"

"I want to kill him myself."

"Him?" McConnell said. "A wolf is an it, Jack, it's not a 'him.'"

"It is to me," Pike said. "He stared at me with that one eye, in that tent, Skins. He was as close to me as you are . . . maybe closer. He's not a dumb animal, Skins, he's smart. He's got a brain. He's devious. He's—"

"He's just a wolf, Jack."

"Yeah, well, I guess I feel he's just as much mine as he is De Roche's."

"Look," McConnell said, "I can understand De Roche's point of view. He was hired to kill the wolf, and we refused to go with him once. Now it looks like we want it for ourselves. He probably doesn't believe that we're not getting paid."

"I don't care what he believes."

"You're so damned stubborn!" McConnell snapped. "Why don't we just ride with him? That way when we kill the wolf, he'll get his money, and you'll get your satisfaction . . . or your revenge . . . or whatever it is you're after."

"All I'm after is that wolf," Pike said. "If you want to ride with De Roche—"

"I'm ridin' with you, Pike," McConnell said.

"Okay," Pike said, "then I don't want to talk about my motives anymore."

"Fine."

85

"We'll leave at first light."

"I'll be ready."

"Good."

"Where are you goin'?"

Pike had started to walk away, and now he turned back and said, "I want to go and check on the boy, and see Jean."

"I'm gonna turn in," McConnell said. "I'll see you in the morning."

Pike waved, and continued walking.

Jean Windham came out of the "doctor's tent" to talk to Pike. She was hugging her arms as if she was cold, and it had nothing to do with the weather.

"How is he?" Pike asked.

"The same," she said. "He hasn't waked up."

"That's good."

She frowned at him.

"If he doesn't wake up, he won't hurt. Maybe . . . maybe he'll heal a bit before he wakes up."

"We're sending a rider to a settlement about two days away," she said. "Black Hole, they call it, but they're supposed to have a doctor."

"Two days," he said. That translated into four days, two there and two back. He hoped that the boy could hang on that long.

"I'm leaving in the morning," Pike said. "I'm going after the wolf."

She looked up at him sharply.

"I'm going to kill him, Jean."

"Pike . . ." she said, and stopped because she didn't know what to say. She came into his arms and he held her for a while. When she stepped back from him she knew what to say. "Don't go."

"I have to."

"Not for me, or for Barry—"

"Yes, for you and for Barry."

"I don't want you to . . . to be hurt, too."

"I won't be."

"Pike—"

"This is something I have to do, Jean," he said. "Please, don't try to talk me out of it."

"All right," she said, putting her hands on his chest, "all right, but be careful."

"I'll be extra careful, Jean," he said, taking her into his arms again, "extra careful."

Chapter Ten

Red Hawk watched as one of his braves was carried into camp by two others. The brave was covered with blood, and from where he stood Red Hawk could plainly see the wounds he had suffered. The brave's squaw was walking with them, wailing. It was clear to all who heard her that her man was dead.

Behind them came the rest of their party, with Dull Knife, the brave who had led them. Several of them also showed similar wounds, though none as serious as those suffered by the dying brave.

"Dull Knife," Red Hawk said. He noticed that Dull Knife was uninjured.

Dull Knife approached Red Hawk and lowered his head, staring at the ground.

"What happened?" Red Hawk asked.

"The devil wolf, and his pack," Dull Knife said. "They attacked us."

"The one-eyed wolf?" Red Hawk asked.

"Yes."

"Did you kill him?"

Dull Knife still had not raised his eyes to look at his leader.

"No," he said.

"Look at me, Dull Knife!" Red Hawk said sternly. Dull Knife reluctantly raised his eyes.

Red Hawk was well respected by his people, and well regarded by his chief. In his late twenties, he was destined someday for the chieftainship of the Snake tribe. He was tall, extremely well built, with startling, slate gray eyes. These eyes were now boring into those of Dull Knife.

"How many were injured?"

"Four," Dull Knife said. "One seriously . . ."

"He will die."

"Yes."

"You were sent out to hunt down the one-eyed wolf and kill him, and his pack," Red Hawk said. "Before they could kill any more of our children."

"They came upon us so quickly," Dull Knife said, "we had no chance—"

"You were looking for the wolves," Red Hawk said. "How could they have surprised you?"

"Red Hawk, I—"

"Where did this happen?"

"It was not far from our first camp, near the twin peaks of—"

"Are you sure it was not near the white settlement?" Red Hawk asked.

"N-no," Dull Knife said, "you strictly forbade us to make any contact with the whites—"

"That would not stop you, Dull Knife," Red Hawk said. "You are greedy."

"Red Hawk, I swear—"

"That's all," Red Hawk said. "I will speak with you later."

"I must—"

"That is all!"

Red Hawk's tone froze Dull Knife, who quickly lowered his eyes. Dull Knife was slight, and much smaller than Red Hawk, and easily intimidated in Red Hawk's presence. He did, however, have some leadership abilities, which was why Red Hawk had charged him with hunting down the wolf. On the other hand, Dull Knife had several times traded with the whites, against Red Hawk's orders. Red Hawk knew now that was a mistake. Dull Knife could not be trusted as a leader, not while he could not control his greed.

Red Hawk turned and went to his teepee. Inside, his wife, Searching Dove, was waiting for him. She had heard what transpired outside.

"Do you want something to eat, husband?"

"No," Red Hawk said. He was angry, but anger never prevented him from noticing what a beautiful woman his wife was. She was younger than he, not yet twenty-three, and they had been husband and wife for a little over two years. She was tall and slender, but full breasted. She had black eyes, a strong nose and chin, and a full, wide mouth. She was the most beautiful woman he had ever seen, and the first time he saw her he swore he would have her. It was a matter of weeks from that point that he had bartered with her father for her hand.

"You are not hungry?"

"I am too . . . angry to be hungry."

She approached him and put her hands against his chest.

"Angry with Dull Knife? That is a waste of your anger, my husband."

"No, my wife, I am angry at myself."

"Why?"

"Because I gave Dull Knife too much responsibility," Red Hawk said.

"You are going after the wolf yourself?"

"Yes," Red Hawk said. "The one-eyed wolf and I are old friends."

"Old adversaries."

"Yes," Red Hawk said, "that, too . . ."

When Red Hawk was a young brave he had gone hunting with just a knife. He had done it to prove a point, to himself and to others. His intention was to bring down a buck, or a buffalo with just the knife. He would not have been disappointed to encounter a dim-witted, slow moving bear.

It was during that hunt that he had run into a young wolf. The animal was very large and powerfully built, dark with gray hair on its back, like ice. The two young warriors froze when they saw each other, and stared. They stared at each other for a long time, and the wolf finally made the first move.

He sprang.

As the wolf was in the air Red Hawk brought his knife around in an arc, and felt it cut, but not deeply. The wolf, despite a wound, landed on his feet and turned to face Red Hawk again. Where his right eye had been there was now a bloody slash, but that didn't stop the animal from springing again. This time Red Hawk tried to duck away, but the wolf's claws caught and tore into his left shoulder.

They faced each other once again, both bleeding from their wounds. The wolf shook his head hard and it rained blood around him. With his remaining eye he refused to blink.

Red Hawk felt the pain, and blood running down his arm and his back, but he never took his eye off the wolf. Abruptly, the wolf turned and walked away, and Red Hawk heaved a sigh of relief.

He then fell face forward into the dirt . . .

Searching Dove's hand touched her husband's scars lightly. There were three of them, from his left shoulder down his back. When they had healed, something

92

inside had not, and Red Hawk was left with limited movement in his left arm. The adversaries had left each other with crippling injuries. She knew her husband had never forgotten, and she knew that her *husband* knew that the wolf never forgot, either.

"I must be the one," he said to her.

"After all this time," she said, "you want to give that devil wolf a second chance to kill you."

"Everyone else thinks of him as a devil wolf," Red Hawk said, "but I know better. I made him bleed. I took his eye."

"And he almost took your arm," she said. "If they had not found you so soon after, you would have died."

Red Hawk moved his left arm, as if to assure himself that it still worked. Looking at him, one would notice that both arms were powerful, with muscles like rocks. However, he was rarely, if ever, able to raise the left arm higher than his shoulder. When he tried, the strength would suddenly leave it. Sometimes he would lose the feeling in that arm, and he would worry until it came back that it might *never* come back.

Red Hawk put his hands on his wife's shoulders and said gently, "All that means it that we have unfinished business, the wolf and I."

He took her into his arms and she rested her head against his chest. When she was within the circle of his powerful arms she felt as if nothing could harm her.

"I will go out after him when the sun comes up," he said. "I will not come back until I have killed him. He has taken enough of our people, our children. I will not come back until I finish what I started that night, when I took his eye."

"Finish what you started," she said against his chest, "and come back to me."

Dull Knife went to his teepee, seething with anger.

93

He knew that physically he was no match for Red Hawk, but he also knew that he was smarter. So he had been trading with the whites when his braves were attacked by the wolves. All that meant was that he was not there to also be injured. The braves who were with him, even the injured ones, knew better than to tell Red Hawk that. That was because all he made from trading with the whites he shared with them.

He knew what Red Hawk would do now, though. He would go after the wolf himself. That suited Dull Knife, because Red Hawk would go after the wolf alone. If the wolf didn't kill him, Dull Knife would find a way to do it himself.

To give his wife something to do, Red Hawk said that he would have something to eat. While she prepared it, he fell deep into thought. He played his first meeting with the wolf over and over again in his mind. He knew that all of the Snake tribe, as well as the Nez Perce, called the wolf a "Devil." Some of them even believed that the wolf was inhabited by a bad spirit. The Nez Perce were against hunting him down. They felt that whatever—and whoever—the wolf killed, it was like a sacrifice to a god.

Red Hawk did not feel that way. He had seen the wolf bleed, and he knew it could be killed. He knew it had to be killed before any more children were killed. White, Snake, Nez Perce children, it didn't matter to Red Hawk. All that mattered was that the wolf should be killed.

All that mattered was that he be the one who killed him.

Ol' One-Eye, the whites called him.

A "devil," a "spirit," his own people called him.

Soon, they would call him a memory.

In the morning, when Pike and McConnell were ready to leave, Locke was waiting to see them off and wish them luck.

"Get that devil," Locke said. "If you get him, I'll give you the money we were going to give De Roche."

Pike and McConnell exchanged a look, and McConnell nodded.

"We don't want the money, Locke," Pike said, "but we'll get the wolf."

"The wolf," McConnell said, to Pike as much as to Locke, "not the devil."

"Right," Pike said, looking at Locke, "it's just a wolf."

Red Hawk hugged Searching Dove and then mounted his pony. He carried a knife, a bow and arrows, and a rifle. From in front of his own teepee, Dull Knife watched.

"Come back to me," Searching Dove said. "Be careful, and come back to me."

"I will be back," Red Hawk said. "I took his eye a long time ago. When I come back I will bring his carcass with me."

After Red Hawk rode out, Dull Knife mounted his own pony. He rode directly to a location where he knew there was a small Nez Perce camp. He knew that the Nez Perce were against killing the one-eyed wolf. They thought the wolf's body was inhabited by the spirit of an old medicine man. When they heard that Red Hawk was going out to kill the wolf, they would stop him.

They would stop him dead.

De Roche broke camp that morning, thinking about Jack Pike. He knew Pike's reputation, but it was easy for a big man to get a reputation. All he had to do was step on some little men. Well, De Roche might not have been tall, but he was no little man, and Jack Pike was not going to add to his reputation by stepping on Anton De Roche.

"If we get in De Roche's way he'll kill us, you know," McConnell said to Pike.

"I know."

"What are we gonna do when he gets in our way," McConnell said, and then added quickly, "and he is goin' to get in our way."

"I don't know," Pike said, after a moment. "I guess we'll have to deal with that when it happens."

Chapter Eleven

Pike and McConnell started their search from the clearing where the wolf had taken young Barry Windham down. They found his tracks there and started following them.

"Biggest wolf prints I ever seen," McConnell commented, looking down at the ground.

"Believe me," Pike said, "he fits them."

"I know," McConnell said, "I've seen him."

"Not like I saw him," Pike said, remembering the night in his tent. "I'd still like to know how he got out of that tent without me seeing him."

"Without bein' a devil wolf, you mean?"

"Yeah," Pike said, "without that."

Red Hawk rode out to where Dull Knife said the wolf pack had attacked his braves. There he picked up the pack's trail. He became even more angry—this time *at* Dull Knife—when he saw that the one-eyed wolf's tracks was not among them. He dismounted to look closely at the ground, but the tracks were not there. He would know them when he saw them, because they would be larger than the tracks of any of the other wolves.

Dull Knife had not told him that the one-eyed wolf

was not among the pack when they attacked. More than likely, that meant that Dull Knife had not even been there when the attack took place. All Red Hawk could do now was track the pack and hope that they would lead him to their leader.

When he returned to camp, he would deal with Dull Knife once and for all.

De Roche crossed the tracks of the pack, but he ignored them. Very often the pack would travel without the leader for days, or weeks. De Roche didn't have that much time. He had to get to the leader before Pike did.

De Roche had been hunting for years on instinct, an instinct he didn't think Pike had. He figured that gave him an edge.

He crossed the pack's trail, ignored it, and continued riding.

Dull Knife rode into the Nez Perce camp. The six Nez Perce braves who inhabited the camp stood up and watched him closely.

"Who among you is leader?" Dull Knife asked.

One of them stepped forward and said, "I am Iron Knife."

"I am Dull Knife."

"An iron knife is sharp," the other brave said.

"A dull knife causes more pain."

Iron Knife was six feet tall, so Dull Knife remained astride his pony.

"What is it you want?" Iron Knife asked.

Dull Knife saw the way they were looking at him. They were all young braves, tall and strong. They were amused by him.

"I am here about the one-eyed wolf," Dull Knife said.

"What about him?" Iron Knife. "He is sacred to us."

"The spirit of the great Shaman lives in the one-eyed wolf," one of the other braves said, and the rest nodded.

"Do you know Red Hawk?" Dull Knife asked.

"He is a great man among your people," Iron Knife said, nodding.

"Yes," Dull Knife said. "He is hunting."

"Why come to us about it?" Iron Knife asked.

"Because," Dull Knife said, "he is hunting the one-eyed wolf. He intends to kill it."

The braves who were standing stiffened, and those who were sitting stood up.

"Why do you tell us this?" Iron Knife asked.

"Because like you, I do not feel that the one-eyed wolf should be killed."

"Is he hunting alone?" Iron Knife asked.

"Yes," Dull Knife said, "he is all alone."

"We cannot let him do this, Iron Knife," one of the other braves said.

"No," Iron Knife said, "we cannot." He looked up at Dull Knife and said, "We thank you for bringing us this information."

"I just do not want to see the animal harmed."

"Do not worry," Iron Knife said, "he will not be."

Pike and McConnell decided not to camp for lunch, but they stopped to water the horses and give them a blow.

"I feel like we're being watched," Pike said.

"I never thought I'd see the day you got spooked," McConnell said.

"Neither did I."

"Come on, Jack," McConnell said, "it's a wolf. After the bears we've been up against—"

"I'd put this wolf up against any of those grizzlies," Pike said.

"A wolf against a bear? You'd lose a lot of money bettin' on something like that."

"Not a wolf against a bear," Pike said, "*this* wolf against a bear."

"You're gettin' spooked again."

"I think that as long as we're hunting this wolf we'd better both be spooked," Pike said. "We'll both live longer, that way."

McConnell lifted his horse's head before the animal drank too much and said, "I guess you're right, Pike, I guess you're right."

"Let's keep moving, then," Pike said. "That might keep us alive longer, too."

Red Hawk continued to follow the trail of the pack, never once wondering what would happen if he suddenly caught up to them.

De Roche continued to rely on his instincts as he searched for Ol' One-Eye. Instead, he found Pike and McConnell. He saw the two men riding below him and stopped to watch them. It was obvious to him that they had not seen him, and he wanted to keep it that way.

De Roche suddenly decided that what he needed to catch this wolf was bait, and what better bait then these two, who knew nothing—in his opinion, of course—about hunting wolves. Wolves could not be hunted the same way you would hunt a deer, or even a bear. Wolves were much smarter than those animals and, De Roche believed, smarter than a lot of people.

De Roche decided to follow Pike and McConnell at a safe distance, hoping that they would either attract Ol' One-Eye's attention, or that they might even stumble upon him by accident. Whichever happened, De Roche would be in a position to take advantage of the situation.

Iron Knife and his braves received from Dull Knife the location from where Red Hawk would start his hunt, and they rode there. Upon their arrival they saw all of the tracks on the ground, and were able to separate them with no problem. The wolf tracks led off one way, while the bulk of the unshod horse tracks led another. There was one horse, however, that was following the tracks of the pack, and that was the way Iron Knife and his Nez Perce braves rode.

At all costs the "spirit wolf" had to be protected.

Ol' One-Eye stood stock still and sniffed the air. He knew now that the mountains and woods were filled with humans, of varying smells and odors. The canny wolf was able to separate the scents. He knew the white man's scent, and he knew the Indian's. He could even separate Snake Indian from Nez Perce, and knew that he was in danger from the Snake Indian.

The two scents that concerned him most were the scent of De Roche, the wolfer. Ol' One-Eye knew the wolfer, who had hunted him many times before.

The other scent was that of Red Hawk. This scent Ol' One-Eye knew, and knew well, from long ago. This was the scent of the human who had taken his eye, and to the wolf there was as much unfinished business as there was to Red Hawk.

Before Ol' One-Eye faced any of these dangers,

however, he wanted to rejoin his pack. He knew that he was at risk alone, and was smart enough to know that there was safety in numbers. Once he had reclaimed his pack, he'd show all of his hunters who the master was.

"Do you see him?" McConnell asked Pike.

"I don't see him," Pike said, "but I sense him. He's above us, in that ridge."

"Been following us a while," McConnell said. "I wonder why? He's the wolfer, not us."

"Bait," Pike said.

"Us?"

Pike nodded.

"That makes sense . . . I guess," McConnell said.

"This way, he also knows where we are, just in case we find the wolf before he does."

"And we know where he is."

"He probably doesn't think we know he's there," Pike said. "I think he has less respect for people than he does for wolves."

"I know a lot of people I respect less than wolves," McConnell said, "but I know what you mean. What do you suggest we do about him?"

"Nothing."

"Nothin'?"

"Like you said, we know where he is, and we have an edge, because he thinks we don't."

"If that didn't sound so confusing I might agree with you."

"Skins—"

"All right, all right," McConnell said, "I was just kiddin'. All right, so we let him follow us. What happens when we find the wolf?"

"I guess we'll just have to wait and see."

"That's just what I like," McConnell said, "surprises . . . lots of them."

"There's a lot of them coming up," Pike said, "that's for sure."

Red Hawk saw the white men, but was confident that they had not seen him.

There were three of them, two travelling together, and one following the two from higher up. Red Hawk was on a similar ridge, but opposite the third man, and a bit lower. He followed for a while, trying to determine what the whites were doing. At first he thought that the third was hunting the first two, but then it appeared that he was just following them.

It also became obvious that the first two were following tracks on the ground. It was then that he decided that all three must be doing the same thing he was doing, tracking the wolf—or perhaps they were tracking *wolves*. In either case, ultimately they were all after the same thing, and it had become important to Red Hawk that he be the one to kill the one-eyed wolf. As far as the rest of the pack was concerned, he was content to leave them to the three whites.

He continued to follow, attempting to identify the men. He decided that he knew who the third one was, from his size and the way he dressed. Red Hawk knew of De Roche, the wolfer, and decided that was who it was.

The other two were more difficult, but Red Hawk then noticed the size of one of them. The first white, the biggest, was larger even than himself. In fact, he was probably the largest white man he had ever seen. He had heard of such a man, he who the Crow called He-Whose-Head-Touches-The-Sky. He knew the white

103

man's name, if he could just remember . . .

Then it came to him. Pike was his name.

Red Hawk had heard of Pike, but had not ever dealt with him. He knew what to expect from De Roche, but not from Pike and the other man. He also knew that he disliked De Roche intensely, and De Roche felt that way about all Indians, no matter what tribe they were from.

A plan started to form in Red Hawk's mind as he continued to follow the three whites.

As darkness began to fall Pike and McConnell decided to camp.

"If De Roche wants to stay hidden he's gonna have to make a cold camp," McConnell pointed out as he started a fire.

"Good," Pike said, "let him freeze his ass off."

"Maybe one of us should go up there and—"

"Let's just leave him alone for a while, Skins," Pike said, interrupting his friend.

"It just irks me to let him think we don't see him," McConnell complained. "I hope he's better at tracking wolves than he is at following men."

De Roche would have preferred to light a fire, but he was accustomed to cold camps, and was prepared for it. He had some dried meat to eat, and he had extra blankets. From what he had heard in Fort Hall, Pike and McConnell's camp had already been attacked once by wolves at night, and it could happen again. If it did, he would be ready.

By the time darkness began to fall Ol' One-Eye had

caught up to his pack, and he had turned them and headed them back toward the settlement, back the way Pike and McConnell were camped.

Red Hawk saw the whites all making camp, but he did not stop. He continued to ride on ahead, intending to double back and put his plan into effect. If everything worked out as he hoped, he'd be able to get rid of De Roche as well as the wolf.

That would make him extremely happy.

Chapter Twelve

Red Hawk's first warning came from his horse. The animal lifted its head and its nostrils flared as the wolf smell reached it.

"Easy," Red Hawk said, his hand tightening on the horse's mane.

The Snake brave looked around him, but on an almost moonless night it was difficult to see beyond a few feet in front of him.

He had ridden ahead of the white camp. His intention had been to enter the camp from that direction. He had heard much about He-Whose-Head-Touches-The-Sky, and was hoping that Pike would see the wisdom of his plan. Red Hawk wanted Pike and his friend to see to De Roche, while Red Hawk saw to the one-eyed wolf.

Now, however, Red Hawk was in grave danger. His horse was becoming more and more skittish, harder to control. This indicated to Red Hawk that it was more than one wolf the animal was smelling. It was difficult to manage the horse with one hand, but Red Hawk was holding his rifle in the other and dared not let *that* go.

Finally, the horse reared, and Red Hawk's grasp on the mane came loose. The Snake brave fell hard to the ground, but he managed to hold onto the rifle. The horse, however, had run off in terror, and Red Hawk was left afoot with a pack of wolves approaching.

"Hear that?" Pike asked.

"What?" McConnell said, lifting his head.

"A horse."

"I don't hear a horse—"

"Shh!" Pike said.

They listened together, but now Pike heard nothing. He could have sworn that he heard a horse in terror.

"What is it?" McConnell asked.

"I thought I heard a horse," Pike said. "No, I'm sure I heard a horse, and it was . . . screaming."

"Things echo out here," McConnell said. "It could have come from anywhere."

"Maybe . . ." Pike said.

Red Hawk regained his feet and held the rifle in both hands. He stood stock still, listening intently. The only thing that might keep him from being surprised was his ears. It would be difficult for a pack of wolves to approach him without making a sound.

That is, if the whole pack approached. If only the one-eyed wolf came after him, he was going to have to be very quick with the rifle. He would rather have relied on his bow, which he was more accurate with, but when he fell off the horse the bow, which was slung across his back, had snapped cleanly in two and now lay useless on the ground. Now he lowered the quiver of arrows to the ground, as they were no good without the bow.

His hands were sweating on the rifle. He had taken the weapon off a white man who had tried to kill him, and had never become very proficient with it. He had taken it because he felt that the rifle might be the better weapon to kill the one-eyed wolf with.

He could have started walking, but he felt sure the wolves were coming and he didn't want to start walking, because he might start running. If the wolves sensed he was afraid, they would swarm over him without caution. He had to stand his ground and show them courage. A foe who was not afraid of them might confuse them and give him a chance to take a few of them with him before they killed him.

Hopefully, he'd be able to put a bullet into the heart of that one-eyed wolf before the pack pulled him down.

His heart pounded as he thought of that one-eyed wolf . . .

Ol' One-Eye moved the pack forward slowly. They had all smelled the horse and the man, and it was all he could do to keep them from charging. He wanted them to move forward carefully. He knew that the foe who was just ahead of them was the hated one who had taken his eye, the only foe who had ever caused him intense pain.

Ol' One-Eye's heart began to race as he anticipated once again tasting his hated foe's blood . . .

"Now I hear it," McConnell said.

"Yes," Pike said.

They both heard a horse approaching at a gallop, and they stood up, their rifles in their hands. When the horse broke into camp they saw that it was a riderless Indian pony. They both lowered their rifles to the ground and moved forward to intercept the animal, which was wild-eyed with fear.

"Look at him," Pike said, holding the animal by the mane, "he's in terror."

"He's running from that pack of wolves," McConnell said, patting the animal's neck. "What else could it be?"

"Where's his rider?"

"Maybe they got him already."

"And maybe not," Pike said. "Hold him."

McConnell watched as Pike went and collected his rifle.

"What are you gonna do?" he asked.

Pike returned to the horse, grabbed a handful of mane, and mounted him.

"I'm going to see where his rider is."

"You can't ride him, he's terrified," McConnell said.

"No time to saddle up, Skins," Pike said. "You do that and follow me."

"Pike, no—" McConnell said, but his friend whipped the horse around with a powerful tug and was off.

"Shit!" McConnell said, and ran to saddle his horse.

From his vantage point De Roche could see what was going on, but didn't understand it. An Indian pony had run into their camp, and Pike had quickly mounted it and ridden it back the way it had come. McConnell was now saddling up, apparently to follow. De Roche decided that some Indian had either fallen off his horse, or been attacked by wolves. Certainly nothing to cause him any concern. It was obvious that Pike and McConnell would have to return to their camp. De Roche also knew that there was no chance they were going to catch that one-eyed wolf at night. The beast was just too smart for that.

He decided to stay where he was, and wait.

Red Hawk could hear them now. They were out

there, among the trees, and they could probably see him. If he fired blindly he might hit one, but he'd also probably spook the others into action. He stood his ground and waited for them to show themselves.

It took all of Pike's strength in his left arm to force the pony back the way it had come. If there was a chance that its rider was still alive, he might need help . . . and there might even be a chance that he'd get a shot at the one-eyed wolf.

When he saw them it was as if they were moving in slow motion.

The one-eyed wolf showed himself first, but he did not charge Red Hawk. Instead, the pack appeared behind him, and it was they who charged him. It appeared as if the leader was just going to watch.

He raised the rifle to take a shot at his old foe, but suddenly the wolves were moving faster and faster, and one of them was already upon him. As it leaped he tried to bring the rifle around, but knew there was not going to be enough time.

And then there was a shot . . .

When Pike saw the Indian, he saw the wolves at the same time. The horse was trying to shy away, so Pike dropped to the ground, pointed his rifle and fired. His shot caught the first wolf in midair, tossing its body aside.

The Indian took advantage of the extra time, aimed his rifle and fired, killing a second wolf.

Pike drew his Kentucky pistol and ran forward, firing a third time. After firing it he dropped it, then

111

reversed the rifle, holding it by the barrel.

The Indian, seeing this, did the same and they stood back to back as the wolves circled around them.

"They don't realize that we have to reload," Pike told the Indian, "but soon they'll get brave and be on us."

"While he watches," Red Hawk said.

Pike didn't have to be told who the Indian was talking about. He could see the one-eyed wolf watching them.

"Pike is my name."

"Red Hawk."

"I've heard of you."

"And I, you."

There was nothing else to say, so they watched the wolves intently.

"We've got one chance," Pike said.

"What is that?"

"I have a friend following me," Pike said, "but what would happen if we charged them instead of waiting for them to charge us?"

"It might confuse them."

"It might also get us killed," Pike said, "but at least something would happen."

"Then we should do it."

"All right," Pike said. "Swing hard and with bad intentions . . . now!"

At the same time they sprang at the wolves, swinging their rifles. Pike felt the jolt up to his shoulders as he hit one of the wolves in the head. The animal gave out a satisfying squeal of pain.

Behind him Red Hawk also swung, catching a wolf in the side and knocking it off balance. He swung again, striking the animal a second time, and it turned and ran.

At that same moment McConnell came into sight, aimed his rifle and fired, downing a wolf.

Abruptly, Ol' One-Eye turned and ran into the darkness, and the remainder of the pack followed.

There were four dead wolves left behind, three shot and one which had died from Pike's blow to the head. Pike had either missed when he fired his pistol, or had simply wounded one of them.

McConnell joined Pike and they both turned to look at the Indian.

"Skins," Pike said, making the introductions, "this is Red Hawk, of the Snake tribe. Red Hawk, my friend, Skins McConnell."

"Your arrival was fortunately timed," Red Hawk said in perfect English.

"You speak English very well," McConnell said.

"I learned from a white missionary."

"You'd better come back to our camp with us," Pike said.

"I do not have a choice," Red Hawk said, spreading his hands.

They retrieved his broken bow, his arrows, his powder horn and possibles bag—both of which he'd need if he was going to use the rifle as anything but a club—and they all walked back to camp.

Chapter Thirteen

When they returned to camp McConnell checked on Pike's horse, and on their pack mule, just in case the pack had come this way. Pike and McConnell went to the fire, where they examined the damage to their weapons.

Red Hawk's bow had been snapped in two. Given time, Red Hawk could fix it, until he could make another one.

Red Hawk's rifle was none the worse for wear, but Pike's had a crack in the wooden stock.

"The wolf I hit must have had a hard head," Pike said.

"Can you fire it?" Red Hawk asked.

"I think so," Pike said. "I'll put a new stock on it when I have the time."

McConnell came to the fire and said, "The animals are all right. Red Hawk, I found your pony."

"Where?"

"He was just standing next to Pike's, plumb out of breath and looking a little wild-eyed. I guess he felt he'd be safe with Pike's horse and the mule."

"Is he injured?"

"Not a mark."

"That is good," he said. "I can always make another bow, but a good pony is harder to find."

"We've got some coffee here. Have you ever acquired a taste for it?" Pike asked.

"I have not," Red Hawk said, "but I know it is hot. I will have some."

"We'll all have some," McConnell said. "Let me get another cup, Red Hawk, and then you can tell us what you're doin' out here."

De Roche couldn't believe his eyes. Not only had Pike and McConnell brought an Indian into their camp, but it was Red Hawk himself. De Roche hated Indians in general, and Red Hawk in particular.

If Pike and Red Hawk were to join forces . . .

"I believe I am here for the same purpose that you are," Red Hawk said. "I am hunting the one-eyed wolf."

"That's why we're here, all right," McConnell said. "He injured a little boy at Fort Hall, a boy my partner had become very fond of."

"It is the killing of the children that has sent me after him, also," Red Hawk said.

"I thought your people considered the wolf sacred," Pike said.

"The Nez Perce think that way," Red Hawk said, "that he is a spirit wolf, and yes, even some of my people believe so, but I know differently."

"How?" Pike asked.

"I know he can bleed," Red Hawk said, "because it was I who took his eye, and he did this to me." He turned and showed them the scars on his shoulder and back. Pike had noticed them before, and wondered if

116

they had been acquired in battle. "So you see, we are old friends, and old foes. We have crippled each other."

"Crippled?" McConnell asked. "You didn't look too crippled back there."

Red Hawk explained about the limitations of his left arm.

"I would not tell this to any white man," he added, "but I know of you, Pike, and you both saved my life from the pack."

"It didn't look like your old foe was playing fair," McConnell said, "sending the pack after you instead of taking you on himself."

"Yes," Red Hawk said, "it would seem the one-eyed wolf simply wants me dead, where I feel that it must be me who kills him."

McConnell looked from Red Hawk to Pike and back and said, "We may have a problem there."

"We have another, also," Red Hawk said. "There is a man following you, watching you."

"De Roche," Pike said.

"You know De Roche?" Red Hawk asked. "And you know he is following you?"

"We've met," Pike said, "and I don't like him, but at least if he's following us we know where he is."

"De Roche is a bad man," Red Hawk said.

"On top of that he's been hired to kill that wolf," McConnell said, "and he won't want any of us gettin' in his way."

"Then you are right to let him follow you," Red Hawk said, "but I have a plan in mind."

"What plan?"

They listened as Red Hawk suggested that Pike and McConnell take care of De Roche while he, Red Hawk, went after the wolf.

"I don't like that plan," Pike said.

"Why not?" Red Hawk asked.

"First of all," Pike said, "what do you mean by 'take care of?'"

"Kill him."

"I have no desire to kill De Roche," Pike said, "not unless he forces me to."

"Why else do you not like my plan?"

"Because I feel the same way as you," Pike said. "I want to be the one to kill the one-eyed wolf."

Pike told Red Hawk about his two encounters with the wolf, the second one in the tent, and then told him the whole story of how Barry Windham was injured by the wolf, who had also killed the boy's father.

"It seems we both have a claim on the wolf's life," Red Hawk said, "but I would say that mine is a greater claim."

Red Hawk looked pointedly at McConnell, who shrugged and looked at McConnell.

"I'm sorry, Pike, but I'd have to agree with him on this one."

Pike looked at them both and said, "In any case, I want to be there when the wolf is killed. I want to see it myself."

"My friend seems to think there is more to this wolf than meets the eye."

"What do you mean?"

"I mean he feels a little the way the Nez Perce feel—" McConnell said, but Pike cut him off.

"That's not right, at all," Pike said. "I'm just . . . there are some things that can't be explained."

"He is not a spirit wolf," Red Hawk said.

"I know that," Pike said, but to McConnell he didn't sound quite convinced.

Red Hawk looked at Skins and said, "Would you be able to take care of De Roche?"

"If you mean by killin' him, no," McConnell said,

118

shaking his head, "but I wouldn't mind puttin' him out of commission for a while."

"How?" Red Hawk asked.

"Let me worry about that," McConnell said. He looked at Pike and said, "What do you think?"

"We wouldn't be having to look over our shoulder for him," Pike said. "That can only be a plus."

"Agreed," McConnell said.

"Yes," Red Hawk said.

"When?" McConnell said.

"Well," Pike said, "we know where he'll be tonight."

"Yeah," McConnell said, "right."

Red Hawk nodded, and none of them looked up at the ridge De Roche was camped on.

They split the watch into three, and made sure that McConnell took the first. When he woke Pike for the second watch, he took his blanket into the shadows to make it look as if he was turning in. Instead, he took his rifle and knife and started for the ridge. As high as De Roche was, it would take him some time to work his way up there. If De Roche was watching, he'd think that McConnell had taken his watch and had gone to sleep.

Of course, since De Roche was alone, he might be asleep himself. If that was the case, it suited McConnell just fine.

Pike took his watch and used the time to think about Red Hawk. From the story the Snake brave told, Pike had to admit to himself that the red man might have a more prior claim on the wolf than he did. Still, he couldn't help thinking that if Barry Windham were here it might be a different story, and he *was* sort of representing the boy.

He heard a movement behind him and turned quickly to find Red Hawk walking toward him.

"It's not time for your watch yet," Pike said. "Still a couple of hours to go."

"I am not sleepy," Red Hawk said. He sat down opposite the fire, and Pike noticed that the Indian avoided looking into the fire to preserve his night vision.

"Yeah," Pike said, "knowing that Ol' One-Eye is out there looking for us makes it kind of hard to feel sleepy, don't it?"

"Yes."

Pike looked at Red Hawk and said, "Ol' One-Eye. That's what we call him."

"It is as good a name as any."

Pike poured two cups of coffee and handed one to Red Hawk.

"What do your people call him?"

"Many things," Red Hawk said. "Some say Spirit Wolf, some say Devil."

"What do you call him?"

"A wolf," Red Hawk said, "just a wolf."

"How old were you when you tangled with him?"

"Maybe eighteen years," Red Hawk said, using the white man's measure of time.

"I was thinking," Pike said, "this must be a pretty old wolf."

"Yes."

"How old would you say?"

"When I was a boy," Red Hawk said, "I heard stories about a big wolf with gray hairs on his back. In the moonlight, they say the hair glistens like ice."

"That's him," Pike said. "The same wolf you heard about as a boy, do you think? Or an offspring?"

"The same wolf whose eye I took," Red Hawk said, "that is all I know for sure. Beyond that . . ."

"Yeah," Pike said, "beyond that . . ."

De Roche couldn't sleep. It was often that way when he was on the hunt. Sometimes, he'd go days at a time without sleep, and would feel none the worse for wear for it.

He watched the camp below him, saw the watch change. Now he was watching as Pike and Red Hawk sat together at the fire. A white man and a red man, sitting together, sharing coffee. He couldn't understand that. How could Pike stand the smell of him?

He picked up his rifle and held it lightly in his hands. From here he was sure he could pick off Red Hawk. Wouldn't that be a feather in his cap, killing that buck? De Roche laughed to himself. He had made a joke without meaning to.

A feather in his cap, he thought as he sighted down the barrel of his rifle. One shot, in the red man's back.

"Hold it," a voice behind him said.

De Roche froze.

"Put the rifle aside, De Roche," McConnell said.

"Is that you, McConnell?"

"It's me."

"Joining forces with that red savage against me?" De Roche asked. He still had not put his rifle aside.

"Let's just say that we're fixing it so that we don't have to worry about you shooting us in the back."

"I wouldn't do that to you, *mon ami*."

"Oh no? Whose back were you just sighting down on?" McConnell asked.

"Red Hawk's," De Roche said, "not Pike's."

"Red Hawk this time, Pike next time. Hand the rifle back . . . now!"

De Roche hesitated, then did as he was told. He held the rifle by the barrel and passed it back so McConnell could grab it. McConnell toyed briefly with the idea of having De Roche throw his weapon off the ridge, but decided against it. With the pack in the area, they might need every weapon they had.

"All right," McConnell said, "time to make a fire, my friend. We're gonna be here for a while."

"Look," Red Hawk said.

Pike looked at Red Hawk and then looked up to where he was pointing, at the ridge. He saw an orange glow.

"A fire," Pike said.

"Yes."

"McConnell has him," Pike said, standing up. That was the only explanation for the fire.

"It will be dawn soon," Red Hawk said. "We will leave then."

"Yes," Pike said.

"The kill must be mine, Pike," Red Hawk said, also standing. "We must agree on that."

"Must we?"

"Yes," Red Hawk said, "we must."

Pike turned and faced Red Hawk. He was several inches taller than the Snake brave, but would not have wanted to tangle with him hand to hand under any conditions. Red Hawk was solidly built, without the muscles that Pike possessed, but imposing nevertheless.

"I'll tell you what we can agree on, Red Hawk," Pike said, finally.

"What's that?"

"That you get the first shot at the wolf," Pike said. "If you miss, then it becomes my turn."

Now Red Hawk examined Pike for a few moments, thinking it over.

"Very well," he said, "agreed."

"Good."

"But . . . if you miss, the next shot belongs to me," Red Hawk said.

"We alternate the shots, eh?" Pike asked. "That could go on forever."

"It will not," Red Hawk said.

"It won't?"

"No," Red Hawk said, "I do not intend to miss the first time."

"Red Hawk," Pike said, "you've already had the first shot."

Red Hawk smiled without showing any teeth and said, "So have you."

As the dawn came Pike and Red Hawk saw to their animals. In the early daylight Red Hawk checked his pony for injuries and found that McConnell had been right. There were none.

Pike saddled his horse, then saw to McConnell's animal, to make sure he was secure and would still be there when McConnell came down from the ridge with De Roche.

As Pike untied the pack mule Red Hawk asked, "Will you leave your friend some supplies?"

"Not necessary," Pike said. "He'll have De Roche's supplies."

Red Hawk looked up at the ridge and asked, "What will he do with De Roche?"

"I don't know."

"He should kill him."

"If you want him dead," Pike said, "you'll have to do it yourself . . . later."

"Yes," Red Hawk said, "maybe I will."

Pike looked up at the ridge and saw McConnell briefly. He stood, waved and then disappeared from sight.

"All right, Red Hawk," Pike said, "let's get this hunt going."

"What are you going to do now?" De Roche asked.

He was seated at the fire, his hands tied behind his back. McConnell, having just waved to Pike, walked over and sat opposite him.

"We'll have a little early morning conversation, De Roche," he said, "and then we'll go down and get my horse."

"And then what?"

"I don't know," McConnell said, shrugging. "We'll have to decide that when the time comes. Meanwhile, what shall we talk about?"

Chapter Fourteen

Pike and Red Hawk went back to the area where Red Hawk had been attacked. They found the tracks of the pack laid down in a haphazard fashion and it was Red Hawk who was finally able to sort them out and identify the tracks of Ol' One-Eye. They started to follow the pack leader's tracks, and before long the other tracks came together.

"They are following him," Red Hawk said. Pike noticed that Red Hawk also referred to Ol' One-Eye as "him" rather than "it."

"But to where?"

Red Hawk didn't answer, because he didn't know any more than Pike did where the one-eyed wolf was taking his pack. All Pike cared about was that the tracks were leading away from Fort Hall. He wondered how Barry and Jean Windham were doing.

Red Hawk had been examining the ground, and Pike was deferring to the Snake brave as the superior tracker. The red man remounted his pony and said, "We should proceed."

*   *   *

"All right," McConnell said to De Roche, "stand up."

"With my hands tied?" De Roche said.

"Do the best you can."

It had been a couple of hours since Pike and Red Hawk left, and McConnell figured it was time to go down and reclaim his horse. He still didn't know what he was going to do with De Roche.

"Where are we going?" De Roche asked after he struggled to his feet.

"You ask too many questions."

Suddenly, De Roche started laughing.

"What's so funny?"

"You don't know what to do with me, do you?" the Frenchman asked. "I bet if Red Hawk was up here he'd just kill me to get me out of the way."

"You'd win that bet," McConnell said.

"So why don't you kill me?"

"I have nothing against you, De Roche," McConnell said. "I don't like you, but to me that's not reason enough to kill you."

"And the money you will get for killing ze wolf?"

"There is no money, De Roche."

"You still expect me to believe that? After this?" De Roche said, indicating his bound hands.

"Like you said, De Roche," McConnell said, "I'm tryin' to keep you out of the way."

"For how long?" De Roche asked. "How long can you keep me tied up?"

"You keep askin' questions," McConnell said, "and I just might kill you."

"Bah," De Roche said, "you do not have the nerve."

"You're confusing lack of nerve with lack of reason," McConnell said, "but you keep talkin' and you might just give me a reason."

McConnell untied De Roche's hands, then stepped back and pointed his rifle at him.

"Pack up your gear, De Roche," he said, "and let's get a move on."

"I don't think you will be wanting to move along just yet, my friend," De Roche said.

"And why is that?"

"Look down there."

From his vantage point McConnell could not see down below, while De Roche could. He moved now so he could see what De Roche was talking about. What he saw made him less than happy. In the camp he and Pike had made were now at least six Indians.

"Nez Perce," De Roche said.

McConnell saw that De Roche was correct.

"They have your horse and supplies."

"So I see," McConnell said. "I wonder if they're just a hunting party, or if they're on somebody's trail."

"Like who? The wolf?" De Roche asked.

"The Nez Perce think the wolf is sacred, don't they?" McConnell asked.

"That is right."

"Then they're not hunting the wolf," McConnell said. "Maybe they're hunting the hunters."

"Us?" De Roche asked.

"We're safe up here for now," McConnell said, "but if they follow the trail Pike and Red Hawk are leaving . . ."

"Your friend Pike is in a lot of trouble," De Roche said. "What are you going to do now?"

McConnell continued to look down at the Nez Perce, while keeping De Roche at bay, and said, "I don't know, yet."

*   *   *

127

Down below Iron Knife watched as his five braves went through the camp.

"A horse, a mule, and many supplies," one of his braves said.

"Any weapons?"

"None."

"Two horses left camp," another brave said, "one Indian, one white."

"Red Hawk has joined forces with a white man," Iron Knife said, "but why have they left the white man's supplies behind?"

The other braves had no answers and watched their leader to see what he came up with.

"Since there is another horse here, Red Hawk must have joined forces with two whites," Iron Knife surmised. He looked around, saying, "The other white must still be near here."

"Shall we look for him, Iron Knife?"

"No," Iron Knife said, "we must continue on. It is more important to stop Red Hawk before he can kill the spirit wolf."

"What will we do with all the supplies?" a brave asked. It was obvious that most of the braves saw this as booty and wanted to keep it.

"Pack the mule and we will take it and the supplies with us," Iron Knife ordered.

"It will slow us down," a brave said. His name was Strong Hand and he was a particularly greedy sort. "Why not have two of us take the supplies along while the rest ride ahead?"

"We will dump the supplies somewhere," Iron Knife said, "and release the mule."

"But—" Strong Hand started. Iron Knife cut his objection off with a sharp hand gesture.

"And the horse?" another brave asked.

128

"Release it now. If there is another white near here, he will not be much danger to us on foot."

The five braves saw to their leader's instructions, while the two white men watched from above.

"It looks like you're on foot, my friend," De Roche said, grinning at McConnell.

"No, my friend," McConnell said, grinning back, "you are."

De Roche lost his grin in a scowl.

"You would not make me walk."

"Sure I would."

"You would not leave me afoot without a weapon, and supplies. Not with the wolf pack in the area."

McConnell sighed and said, "Now there you're probably right. Shut up for a minute and let me think."

McConnell had to get to Pike and Red Hawk and warn them, before the Nez Perce caught up with them. He couldn't do that while dragging De Roche along. He had two options, either kill the Frenchman or leave him afoot with a weapon and some food and his own cunning to keep him alive. At least afoot De Roche would be no danger to them—no immediate danger.

"All right," McConnell said.

"Good," De Roche said, "untie me."

"You misunderstand me, De Roche," McConnell said. "I'm gonna untie you, all right, but then I'm gonna leave you here."

"Then you might as well kill me."

"I'll leave you a weapon, and some food. Maybe on foot you can find your way back to Fort Hall."

"If you leave me," De Roche said, "I will follow you."

"Do you want me to kill you?" McConnell asked.

"I am simply telling you ze truth, McConnell," De Roche said. "I will not go back to Fort Hall without my wolf."

McConnell shook his head.

"Which way you go after I release you is up to you, then. I can't be concerned with that. I have to reach Pike and Red Hawk ahead of those Nez Perce Indians."

Still holding the Frenchman at bay McConnell began to sort through the supplies. If he was going to have any chance of catching up to Pike and Red Hawk he was going to have to leave most of the supplies behind. That meant leaving De Roche the mule, as well. The pack animal would just slow his progress.

"I'm leaving you the mule and most of the supplies," he said.

"What about a weapon?"

"Wait."

Pike went through De Roche's property thoroughly and found what he thought he would. De Roche owned a Kentucky pistol, and kept it packed away. He probably used it as a back up weapon.

"I'll leave you the pistol."

"Leave my rifle!"

"Sorry."

When he did reach Pike he could give his friend De Roche's rifle, and then Pike wouldn't have to try and use his, with the split stock.

McConnell laid out a blanket, filled it with supplies, then wrapped it up and tied it. He had De Roche saddle his horse and tie the supplies to the saddle.

"Back off," he told the Frenchman, and then mounted the horse.

"McConnell, you cannot leave me."

"Sorry, De Roche," McConnell said, "but I just

130

don't have time for you."

He tossed the Frenchman the unloaded pistol, then the powder horn and possibles bag he'd need to load it. If De Roche intended to ride the mule, he would have to leave most of the supplies behind to do so. A mule was a reliable mountain mount, but there was no way De Roche would be able to keep up with the horse McConnell was riding.

"This is nothing personal, De Roche," McConnell said. "My friend and Red Hawk simply want to see that wolf dead. That is the only profit any of us will see."

"There is something I do not understand."

"What?"

"How can you and Pike join with that red savage against me?"

McConnell made a face at the obvious prejudice in the Frenchman's voice and said, "Remind me to answer that question for you another time."

McConnell wheeled the horse around and started to ride away. De Roche stared at the pistol in his hand, wondering if he could load it quickly enough to shoot McConnell in the back. Probably not.

"I will not forget this, McConnell!" he shouted. "You will pay for this! You and Pike and Red Hawk! You will all pay!"

As McConnell rode away from De Roche he hoped that he had enough time to circle wide of the Nez Perce and get to Pike before they did. If the Nez Perce had somehow learned that Red Hawk and others were hunting Ol' One-Eye, they'd be bound and determined to stop the hunters at all costs. It wouldn't bother the Nez Perce at all to kill a Snake Indian brave and a couple of white men under the most normal of circumstances, but to save their spirit wolf they'd be even more determined.

In the face of the Nez Perce threat, McConnell forgot about De Roche just moments after leaving him on that ridge. Later, he'd realize what a mistake it had been not to kill the Frenchman.

Chapter Fifteen

Pike and Red Hawk stopped to rest their horses by a stream. While Pike watered the animals Red Hawk examined the ground. The stream was only about five or six feet wide, and several inches deep. Red Hawk crossed the cold water to the other side.

"They crossed the stream," he finally said to Pike.

"They're continuing to head away from the settlement," Pike said.

"And away from my camp."

"Where are they headed, then?"

Red Hawk shrugged and came back across the stream to take his pony from Pike.

"Maybe they're not headed anywhere," Pike said, mounting up.

"What do you mean?"

Pike crossed his forearms on his saddle horn and leaned forward.

"You're going to think I'm crazy."

Red Hawk didn't say anything, he just waited.

"What if Ol' One-Eye is just luring us somewhere?"

"To kill us?" Red Hawk asked.

"What else."

If he expected Red Hawk to ridicule his question he was disappointed. The Snake brave seemed to actually be considering its merit.

"There is no doubt in my mind that the wolf is capable of intelligent action," Red Hawk finally said. "He is cunning, and vicious."

"And he's afraid," Pike added.

Red Hawk looked at him sharply.

"Of who?"

"Of you."

"Why do you say that?"

"It's fairly obvious to me," Pike said. "He sent the pack after you and stayed back to watch. He was afraid to attack you himself."

"Because of what happened long ago?"

"What other reason could there be?"

Red Hawk frowned.

"I do not know."

"If he's luring us into a trap, the trap will be sprung by the pack," Pike said. "What we want to do is isolate him from the pack."

"And how do we do that?"

"I don't know," Pike said, "but we're going to have to figure out a way."

They crossed the stream and once again began to follow the trail of the pack.

After they had ridden a few miles Pike asked Red Hawk, "Do you have a woman waiting for you?"

"Yes," Red Hawk said. "My wife. You?"

"A friend," Pike said, after a moment. "The mother of the injured boy."

"You are doing this for her, or for the boy?" Red Hawk asked.

"The boy."

"How old is he?"

"About twelve. When he was very young he saw Ol' One-Eye kill his father. In spite of that, he's grown into a fine lad."

"Seeing your father killed is a terrible experience," Red Hawk said, "and one I share with him."

"How was your father killed?"

"In battle," Red Hawk said, "but I was there to see it."

"How did it affect you?"

Red Hawk took a moment to think, and then said, "I think I grew up faster."

"Is that good or bad?"

"A little of both. After my father's death I went to learn from the missionaries. I wanted to learn as much as possible as quickly as possible. I thought it would make me grow up faster, become a warrior faster. I wanted to be someone my father would have been proud of."

"And are you?"

"Yes."

They rode a little farther before Pike realized that he hadn't asked who his father had been in battle against when he was killed, whites or other Indians.

He decided that it was too late to bring the subject up again.

McConnell went back down to his camp for a brief look. There was nothing to be salvaged, and so he rode on. He followed the tracks of the Nez Perce for a while, and as they became fresher and fresher he started to swing wide of them. De Roche's horse was a good animal, and McConnell began to push him. He was going to have to travel almost twice as far as the Nez Perce in order to get around them and in front of them.

135

Iron Knife called a halt to their progress and turned to look at Strong Hand. The other Nez Perce brave was the same age as Iron Knife. In fact, they played together as children, but as they grew older they also grew apart. Soon, Iron Knife was far ahead of Strong Hand in the eyes of the elders, and Strong Hand resented it.

"Release the mule."

"Let me take some of the supplies off—" Strong Hand began to say, but Iron Knife cut him off.

"Release it, Strong Hand. We have more important things to think about than what you can steal."

Strong Hand felt the eyes of the other braves on him, and wanted to stand up to Iron Knife. He simply did not have the courage.

He released the reins of the mule and one of the other braves slapped the animal on the rump. The mule began to lazily amble off, refusing to be hurried.

Aside from Iron Knife, Strong Hand had been the only other Nez Perce brave to recognize Dull Knife for what he was when he came into camp. That was because Dull Knife and Strong Hand were a lot alike.

When the mule was out of sight Iron Knife started forward again, with the other braves behind him. Strong Hand was taking up the rear.

After they had gone about a mile Strong Hand called out, "Stop."

Iron Knife stopped and turned to look back.

"What is it?"

"I think we are being followed."

Iron Knife looked beyond Strong Hand, but could see nothing.

"All right," he said, finally, "take Running Lake and go—"

"I will go back and check it myself," Strong Hand said. "If you catch up to Red Hawk in my absence, you will need all the men you have."

Iron Knife, certainly not as foolish or gullible as Strong Hand would like to think, squared his jaw and then said, "Very well. Go."

Strong Hand nodded, turned his pony and started back the way they had come.

Iron Knife did not have the time to devote to Strong Hand at the moment. Later he would teach the other brave the folly of daring to think that Iron Knife was so easily fooled.

Strong Hand rode back to the point where he had released the mule and started to follow the animal's trail. It was stupid to allow that much booty to go to waste. He would take what he wanted, secrete it someplace where he could retrieve it later, and then go back and join the others in their hunt for Red Hawk and the spirit wolf.

Spirit Wolf, Strong Hand thought derisively. If the One-Eyed Wolf was inhabited by the spirit of a Shaman, why would it be in any danger from anything human? Let Iron Knife and the others cling to their superstitions, and perhaps die for them. Strong Hand preferred to deal in what was real . . . like the supplies on that mule's back.

McConnell knew he still had a distance to go before he reached a point of even being parallel with the Nez Perce braves, but he thought he heard someone or something coming toward him. He reined in the horse he had "borrowed" from De Roche and listened. Sure enough, something was running toward him. Abruptly, he saw the pack mule coming toward him, and recognized it. It was his and Pike's.

He dismounted and waited for the mule to reach him. The Nez Perce must have released him, figuring it would slow them down, and at the same time keeping it from the whites whose camp they had taken it from.

Examining the mule, McConnell didn't see much missing. Whatever was missing he assumed Pike had taken. The Indians had apparently not taken the time to loot the supplies.

He was digging around in the mule's pack looking for some dried meat when something made him turn just in time to save his life.

Strong Hand saw the mule, and the white man who was going through the pack. Whether or not this was the white man from whom they had taken the pack was irrelevant. All he saw was someone stealing what he felt was rightfully his.

He dismounted, leaving his pony behind, and moved up behind the white man, his knife held firmly in his right hand. He drew the knife up to drive it into the man's exposed back, and then the white man turned, and Strong Hand struck . . .

McConnell brought his right arm up to ward off the blow. He managed to deflect the knife, but took a cut on the arm doing it. He brought his left over the Nez Perce brave's right, striking the man flush on the nose. The Indian staggered back a few steps, shook his head,

138

peppering the ground with bloody drops, and then came forward again.

McConnell's rifle—as well as De Roche's—was on his horse, and he had no time to go for it. He moved away from the mule, circling the Indian, and brought out his own knife.

He could tell by the look on the Indian's face that this would be a fight to the death.

Chapter Sixteen

McConnell could only surmise that this was one of the Nez Perce Indians who had doubled back to steal some of the supplies off the mule. Apparently, the leader had simply wanted to set the animal free, with the supplies on it. This brave, seeing McConnell with the mule, was more than willing to kill for the supplies on the mule's back.

McConnell and the brave traded swipes with their knives while McConnell tried to back his way to his horse. Knife fighting was not one of his favorite sports and it would suit him just fine to reach his rifle and put a ball into the brave's gut.

The Nez Perce, able to decipher what McConnell was trying to do, decided to try a blind rush. He swung his knife wildly and ran toward McConnell, who dropped down and swept his leg through the Indian's, taking the brave off his feet. Strong Hand was quick, however, and rolled away as McConnell tried to stomp him. He continued to roll, intending to come to his feet, but instead he rolled too far, into the path of the mule. The animal reared up, spilling some of the supplies, and when he came down his right forefoot caught Strong Hand on top of the head. The Indian lay still as the mule moved away, his work done.

McConnell saw the blood coming from the brave's head, but he knew that scalp wounds bled profusely. A lot of blood did not mean that the man was dead. He approached cautiously, and when he saw a flash of bone white among the red, he knew what had happened. The Indian's head had crumpled beneath the hoof like an egg shell, and the man was dead.

McConnell put his knife away and reclaimed the mule. He decided to simply tie the animal off so that he could return later to reclaim him. Hopefully, he would not be leaving the beast to his doom. If the wolf pack came back this way, the mule would be helpless.

He left the brave lying where he was, and mentally ticked him off the list of six Nez Perce braves. Now they were down to five. If McConnell could reach Red Hawk and Pike before they did, the odds would be much more even at three-to-five than they would have been at two-to-six.

McConnell hoped there would be no more surprises along the way.

De Roche was blind with anger and hate. He could feel it burning behind his eyes, and in his belly. It was what was going to keep him alive, and fuel him to take his revenge on Pike and McConnell.

After McConnell left, De Roche built a fresh fire. He sat by it and planned his vengeance.

First of all, that wolf was still his. The way De Roche figured the one-eyed wolf, there was no place else he could take his pack for food except this area. To go elsewhere would be a long trip, and he had already tried it once. That was when he and his pack had invaded Pike and McConnell's camp. Ol' One-Eye had come back before, and he would come back again. He would lead Pike and McConnell and their savage on a merry

142

chase, and then lead them right back here, back to Anton De Roche.

Of course, Pike and the others were going to have to survive the Nez Perce, but from what De Roche knew of Pike, and of Red Hawk, he did not think that was going to be a problem.

De Roche laughed to himself at Skins McConnell. The man would have been wiser—much, much wiser— to have killed him. De Roche would now simply wait for them all to come back to him, back within the reach of his vengeance.

When Pike and Red Hawk camped that night they thought that all the danger they were to face was in front of them. As far as they were concerned, Skins McConnell had the rear covered.

Their intention was to split the watch, but as with the night before neither of them could sleep very well.

"If that pack comes into camp," Pike said, "I'd like to be awake to die."

"It is very unusual for a pack of wolves to invade a camp," Red Hawk said.

"This pack is being led by a very unusual wolf," Pike pointed out.

"Yes, it is," Red Hawk said. "I should have killed him when I had the chance."

"All those years ago?" Pike asked. "You were young, Red Hawk, all you wanted to do was come out of that situation alive. Nobody can blame you for that."

"I can."

"And I can blame myself for not killing him when he came into my camp the other night? Blame myself for the boy's injuries. You may want to walk around with that kind of blame on your mind, but I sure as hell don't. I refuse to."

"Do you have a woman?" Red Hawk asked, abruptly changing the subject.

"No," Pike said. "I did . . . once . . . for a while. She was a Crow woman."

If Red Hawk was surprised he did not show it.

"What happened to her?"

"She was killed."

"By who?"

"White men."

"What happened to them?"

"I killed them," Pike said, "all of them."

"How many?"

"Five."

"It must have taken you a long time."

"It did."

"And how much time will you spend trying to kill this wolf?"

"As much as it takes."

"As will I."

Pike guessed that Red Hawk had probably just learned something about him, which was probably what the Snake brave had been after with his questions. That was fair, because just from talking to him Pike was learning things about Red Hawk, things that he liked, and respected. He hoped that Red Hawk felt the same things about him.

If they respected each other, and could depend on each other, then it would be a lot easier to keep each other alive.

Maybe.

Iron Knife ordered his braves to make camp. There was no need to ride through the night, because Red Hawk and his white friend would be camping. They would not be foolish enough to try to hunt the spirit wolf at night. They would be sealing their fates if they did that.

Tomorrow there would be plenty of time to catch up to them.

McConnell decided to keep riding through the night. De Roche's horse was surefooted, and McConnell needed the extra time to catch up to Pike and Red Hawk. He knew that they would be camping tonight, he only hoped that the Nez Perce would also camp. If they did, then he'd definitely be able to bypass them and get to Pike in time to warn him about the danger coming up behind him.

Right now, the danger Pike didn't know about was more deadly than the danger he did know about.

Jean Windham pulled the blanket up to her son's chin. The blanket covered most of the bandages, except for the one along the left side of his face. Luckily, the wolf had never reached his throat, or he would probably already be dead.

The boy was holding on well, she thought. Still, she would feel a lot better when the doctor arrived.

She walked to the front of the tent and stepped outside. She had not spent a night in her own home, or in her own bed, since he had been injured.

Outside, her thoughts turned to Jack Pike. She hoped that he would not be killed by wolves before she got a chance to get to know him. The way he made friends with Barry, that made him a special man to her. Barry had not reacted to any man that way since his father died.

She looked up at the mountain peaks above her and wondered how far Jack Pike would have to go before he would catch up to the one-eyed wolf.

And she wondered what would happen when he finally did.

Pike was thinking about Jean and Barry Windham. After this was over, he promised himself a chance to get to know Jean better before moving on. He also didn't want to leave Fort Hall until he knew the boy was fully recovered.

He looked across the fire at Red Hawk and wondered what the Snake brave was thinking about.

Red Hawk was thinking about Searching Dove, his wife. He was thinking about his position in the Snake tribe. He knew that very soon in his life he would be blessed or burdened with great responsibility, and he hoped that he would be man enough to bear it.

None of that was important, however, as long as the one-eyed wolf was alive. While the wolf was alive that fear would always be there, a bitter taste on his tongue, still fresh despite all the years. The wolf had to be dealt with now, so that he could get on with the rest of his life.

Ol' One-Eye trained that single eye on his old foe, and the other human. He watched Pike and Red Hawk seated at the fire, and thought better of taking the pack into the camp. For one thing, the pack was not as large as it had once been. Recent encounters with men had reduced the pack's number by almost a third.

Ol' One-Eye was going to wait, this time, before attacking. He was going to wait for the right time, the right place, and then he would kill his foe himself, instead of leaving it to the pack.

That was the way it should be.

*   *   *

Barry Windham was dreaming.

He saw his father battling with a big gray wolf. On its hind legs the wolf was even taller than his father was. Barry was screaming, and the blood was streaming down his father's face. Suddenly, another man appeared in the dream, a great big man with a heavy beard.

"Kill it!" Barry shouted. "Kill the wolf!"

The man raised the rifle and fired . . .

Pike looked over at Red Hawk and saw that the brave was sitting up much straighter, listening.

"What is it?"

Red Hawk held up his hand for silence, and Pike gave it to him. Before long he too could hear it. A horse, moving at an unhurried pace.

Abruptly, Red Hawk stood up and melted away into the darkness. Pike thought he knew what the man had in mind, and he simply remained by the fire. He was the bait, and here was one of the instances when he was just going to have to trust Red Hawk to keep him alive.

He listened intently, an itch forming at the small of his back and working its way up higher and higher. He could hear the horse coming closer and closer, and then he heard the sounds of a struggle. He jumped up and ran to help Red Hawk.

When he reached them they were rolling over on the ground. Closed up on each other like that, it was impossible for them to see each other, but Pike could see them both very clearly.

The man Red Hawk was struggling on the ground with was Skins McConnell.

147

Chapter Seventeen

After he managed to separate them, Pike and Red Hawk sat around the fire with McConnell, each with a cup of coffee, and McConnell told them about the six Nez Perce braves who were following them.

"But they are only five now," Red Hawk said when McConnell finished his story.

"That's right."

"And what of De Roche?" Red Hawk asked. "Did you kill him?"

"I didn't," McConnell said.

"Did you leave him tied up?"

"No."

Red Hawk leaned forward and asked, "What did you do?"

"I set him free."

"You set him free?" Red Hawk asked in disbelief. "Why did you do that?"

"Let him explain, Red Hawk," Pike said.

"I left him his mule so he could make his way back to Fort Hall."

"Did you leave him a weapon?" Red Hawk asked.

"That reminds me," McConnell said. He handed Pike a rifle and said, "This is De Roche's. I figured you could use it until you got yours fixed."

"Good," Pike said, accepting the weapon. "Thanks."

"Then you did not leave him armed," Red Hawk said.

"I left him his pistol."

Red Hawk simply stared at McConnell.

"Well," McConnell said, looking at both of them, "leaving him unarmed would have been the same as killing him."

"That is what you should have done."

"I told you once, Red Hawk," McConnell said, "if you want that done you're gonna have to do it yourself. I ain't gonna do your killin' for you."

"I did not ask—"

"Hold it a second," Pike said. "We're not going to get anywhere arguing among ourselves. What's done is done and we'll have to live with it."

"I hope that we can."

"Red Hawk—"

"That's enough," Pike said, cutting them off again. "Let's put this one to rest, at least until later. What are we going to do about the Nez Perce?"

"And how did they know that we were hunting Ol' One-Eye?" McConnell asked.

"They do not," Red Hawk said.

"What do you mean?" Pike asked.

"I mean that they did not know about you when they started out. It is me they are after."

"Well, how did they know that you were hunting the wolf?" Pike asked.

"There is only one way," Red Hawk said. "Dull Knife."

"Who is Dull Knife?" McConnell asked.

Briefly, Red Hawk told them about Dull Knife, who had gone from his childhood to a bitter manhood.

"You think Dull Knife told the Nez Perce that you

were hunting the spirit wolf?" Pike asked. "One of your own people?"

"Is not De Roche one of your people?" Red Hawk asked.

"Point well taken," Pike said. "We both have those among our own people that we don't get along with."

"It is more than that," Red Hawk said. "Dull Knife's bitterness has long ago turned to hatred."

"Why hasn't he tried to kill you himself?" McConnell asked.

"He does not have the courage to face me himself," Red Hawk said. "He would rather kill me this way."

"By having someone else do it for him," McConnell said.

"Yes," Red Hawk said. "If he did it by himself, he would not do it unless he could do it from behind."

"A backshooter," Pike said.

"Yes."

"You'll have to take care of him when you get back," Pike said.

"I intend to."

"Right now," McConnell said, "we've got to figure out what to do with those Nez Perce."

"Tell me," Red Hawk said, speaking to both of them, "do you have a problem with killing Nez Perce."

McConnell almost said that he didn't have a problem killing any Indians, but managed to stop himself.

"No," Pike said, "not save our lives."

"Good," Red Hawk said, "then with your permission, here is what I think we should do . . ."

The next morning they did not break camp. Pike, however, took his horse and walked out of camp with it. Red Hawk and McConnell remained seated at their fire, where they would wait for the Nez Perce to catch up.

From what McConnell had told them they figured that it wouldn't take the Nez Perce more than half a day to catch up to them if they stayed still. Red Hawk's idea was for them to push the issue instead of waiting for the Nez Perce to catch up and attack.

They were going to catch up, but when they did they'd find a surprise.

Iron Knife and his braves broke camp at first light and prepared to move out.

"What happened to Strong Hand?" one of the braves asked aloud.

"Never mind," Iron Knife said. "I will take care of Strong Hand in my own way when we are finished."

The other four braves exchanged glances that said they were glad that they weren't Strong Hand.

"We will move swiftly today and save the spirit wolf, and then I will deal with Strong Hand."

The others nodded and mounted up.

"We could be sitting here for a long time," McConnell said to Red Hawk.

"Not if you are correct about how far behind us they are."

"What if they change direction?"

"Why would they?" Red Hawk said. "They will be following our trail right to here."

"I guess I'm just impatient," McConnell said. "Or maybe I've just screwed up so much lately that I expect to do it again."

"You have not screwed up, my friend," Red Hawk said. "I should not fault you for not wanting to kill a man. You are right in saying you have no reason. I will deal with De Roche myself."

"I appreciate that, Red Hawk, but there still could have been another way to handle it."

"I am afraid that our people think each other savage," Red Hawk said. "Perhaps we are examples that this is not the case."

"Maybe you're right."

Red Hawk looked up at the sky and said, "They should be along any time now."

"I don't know why I'm complaining," McConnell said. "Pike is the one who should be complaining. At least we're comfortable while waiting."

Pike had found himself a spot behind a stand of trees, where he and his horse was safely out of sight. When the Nez Perce arrived, they would expect to see one Snake Indian and one white man, and that's what they would see. Pike had the rifle McConnell had borrowed from De Roche, and his own Kentucky pistol. With any luck, he'd be able to take two of them from their horses before the other three knew what was happening. After that, it would be up to McConnell and Red Hawk.

Meanwhile, while he was waiting for the Nez Perce to arrive he also had to be on the lookout for the wolves. His was not the most desirable job in Red Hawk's plan, but if the ambush worked, it would be worth it.

Iron Knife sent one of the braves on ahead to scout, and pulled his horse to a stop when he saw the brave returning.

"They are just up ahead, Iron Knife," the brave reported.

"How many?"

"Two."

"Are you sure?"

"There are two men, and two horses," the brave said.

"What are they doing?"

"They are just sitting there."

Iron Knife stared ahead.

"Will we attack them?" the brave asked.

"They should not be there."

"What?"

"It is almost midday," Iron Knife said. "Why are they still camped? They should be hunting."

"Maybe there is something wrong with one of them. Or with one of their horses."

"That is possible," Iron Knife admitted, "but it bothers me that they are still camped." The other alternative was that they were somehow waiting for Iron Knife and his men, and setting a trap.

"Then what will we do?" another brave asked.

Iron Knife thought a moment and then said, "Listen carefully . . ."

"I just thought of somethin' uncomfortable," McConnell said.

"What?"

He looked at Red Hawk over his coffee cup and said, "Why are we sittin' here?"

Red Hawk stared at him for a moment, and then said, "I do not understand."

"I mean," McConnell said, "when the Nez Perce get here and see us just sittin' here, what are they gonna think? We're supposed to be out huntin' a spirit wolf and here it is midday, and we're still camped. What would you think if you were in their place?"

"That is a good thought," Red Hawk said, "but one that has come a little late, don't you think?"

154

"Yes," McConnell said, "I do think. In fact, I wish it hadn't come at all. I guess we'll just have to wait and see what happens."

"Yes, I think so, too."

"We seem to be doin' a lot of that, lately," McConnell said.

"A lot of what?"

"Sittin' and waitin'."

"Yes," Red Hawk said, frowning, "it goes against my nature, too."

Pike was beginning to wonder if the Nez Perce would ever show up when suddenly they were there, in a clearing just behind the campsite.

From where he stood he could see the Nez Perce, as well as McConnell and Red Hawk, but they could not see each other.

Pike checked both of his weapons to make sure they were ready to fire. He was all set to put Red Hawk's plan to work, but there was something not right. McConnell had said there would be five Nez Perce braves, and in the clearing, sitting astride their ponies, were only three.

What happened to the other two?

Having two Nez Perce braves running around somewhere unchecked was definitely not part of the plan.

Chapter Eighteen

Pike had to think quickly. There were two Nez Perce unaccounted for. They could be anywhere, and if he fired two shots at the three he could see, the two he couldn't see might kill him.

He had to fire at least once, though, which would leave two Nez Perce for McConnell and Red Hawk to take care of. He would then have to locate the other two before they located him, and he'd only have one shot—the Kentucky pistol—to deal with both of them.

He had to make the decision fast, so he raised his rifle as the three Nez Perce started forward toward the camp, sighted down on one of them, and fired.

As Iron Knife gave the signal to move forward, there was a shot. The brave to his left was literally flung from his horse and thrown to the ground. Iron Knife shouted, and he and the remaining Nez Perce brave charged the camp. He would leave the hidden white man to the other two braves.

As the shot sounded both Red Hawk and McConnell jumped up in time to see Iron Knife and the other brave ride into camp.

Red Hawk recognized Iron Knife. He pointed to the other brave and said, "That one is yours."

Neither of them paused to wonder why Pike had only fired once, or why there were only two Nez Perce charging them.

Things began to happen too quickly to ask questions.

Pike put his rifle down, not bothering to even try and reload. He looked around him quickly and saw them. They were coming at him from two different directions, and they were on foot.

As they came closer to him he extended his Kentucky pistol and fired. The ball struck one of the braves in the chest, knocking him back several steps before he fell.

The second brave, knife in hand, leaped at Pike. Pike swung with the pistol and missed, and went down with the weight of the Indian atop him. He never even had the chance to produce his own knife.

They rolled around for a few seconds, and then came to a stop with the brave on top. He brought the knife down toward Pike's throat, but Pike caught the wrist in his hand, checking the downward progress of the knife. He brought his other hand up and pushed the palm beneath the brave's chin, forcing the man's head back. The brave gripped Pike's wrist with his other hand, trying to loosen the grip. Pike knew that if he could keep pushing he might just snap the brave's neck.

The brave was neither as big or as muscular as Pike, but Pike could feel the power in the man's slighter frame. The brave's knife hand was at a standstill, though. The red man just couldn't push down against the power of Pike's hand.

Pike continued to push the man's chin and head up, and finally the brave decided to break the tableau. He rolled away from Pike, away from the pressure under his chin. Free of the Indian's weight Pike scrambled to his feet and pulled his own knife.

Now they were on much more even terms.

McConnell swung his rifle around to fire at the advancing Nez Perce brave, but the Indian was riding low on his horse, and was effectively shielded by the animal's neck. McConnell did not want to waste his shot on the horse, so he moved forward to meet the Indian's charge.

None of the Nez Perce had rifles, and because Red Hawk had recognized Iron Knife, the Snake brave left his rifle by the fire. Instead, he pulled his knife and moved toward Iron Knife.

Iron Knife could see that Red Hawk had recognized him, and that pleased him. The two braves had known and disliked each other for a long time, but they also respected each other. It would be a feather in the cap for one to kill the other, especially hand to hand.

Iron Knife dropped down from his pony to face Red Hawk.

Pike was not a knife fighter, but he had an advantage over the Nez Perce brave, and that was his superior reach. His arms were so much longer that even when he darted in to swipe at the other man with his knife, he was not within the brave's reach. Finally, the brave seemed to realize this, and he decided to throw caution to the wind. He came right at Pike with his knife flashing. Pike managed to wrap the man's knife arm up in his free arm, his wrist ending beneath the man's armpit. Their arms were effectively intertwined, rendering the brave's knife arm useless. Pike pulled the brave to him and thrust forward with his knife. The brave tried to use his other hand to ward off the thrust, but he was too slow. The point of Pike's knife struck the man's skin just below the sternum. The knife—propelled by Pike's power—penetrated to the hilt, and a look of shock came over the brave's face. Pike held him there until he felt the life drain out of him, then disentangled his arm, pulled his knife free, and let the man fall to the ground.

Quickly, he checked the other brave to make sure he was dead, then rushed to the camp to help Red Hawk and McConnell, if they needed it.

McConnell sidestepped, so that the brave's pony went by him, but he reached up and wrapped his arms around the brave's right leg. With no saddle to hang onto, the brave slid right off his horse and hit the ground with a hard thud. McConnell backed off, picked up his fallen rifle, and managed to get off his shot as the brave was struggling to his feet. The force of the ball knocked the brave onto his back, where he lay still.

Red Hawk and Iron Knife faced each other as it suddenly became quiet.

Pike reached McConnell and they both studied the two braves, wondering if they should step in.

"This is Iron Knife, of the Nez Perce," Red Hawk said to them.

Iron Knife straightened and looked at the two white men.

"My braves?"

"They're all dead," Pike said.

Iron Knife nodded at the news and then said, "And I am next? Which of you will shoot me."

"They will not shoot you, Iron Knife," Red Hawk said. "I have been told that I must do my own killing, so I will kill you myself."

Iron Knife shrugged.

"You will try, but I will kill you, Red Hawk, and then your white friends will kill me, and once again only the white man will be left. Why not join with me? We will wipe them out."

"And then you will kill me when I am not looking," Red Hawk said.

Iron Knife stiffened.

"Women kill from behind," he said, "old women. No, I will kill you from the front."

"Then do it now, Iron Knife," Red Hawk said.

"Wait a minute—" Pike said, but Red Hawk cut him off.

"This has been coming for a long time," he said to Pike and McConnell. "Please, do not interfere."

"And what are we supposed to do if he kills you?" McConnell asked.

"That will be up to you," Red Hawk said.

McConnell looked at Pike, who simply shrugged. Both men then backed off and began to reload their weapons, just in case there were more Nez Perce around—or in case the wolves chose that moment to strike.

Red Hawk and Iron Knife circled each other for a few moments before one or the other started to feint forward. Pike watched both men and admired the way they handled their knives. These were two Indians who knew what they were about when it came to knife

161

fighting. However this battle came out, it would be an education.

Ol' One-Eye watched patiently. He had fought with his own kind enough times to recognize when it was happening to another species. Two of the humans were fighting for leadership. Ol' One-Eye watched, aware that knowing as much as you could know about your foes was important.

As they feinted in and out Pike could see that both braves were amazingly quick. Given his choice, he wouldn't have wanted to face either of them with a knife.

Red Hawk was the larger of the two, by a couple of inches and probably twenty pounds, but that did not make Iron Knife a small man. Also, in the matter of quickness they seemed even, but in the matter of speed Pike might have had to give the nod to the smaller of the two, Iron Knife. All that meant in this case, however, was that if Iron Knife had chosen to run, Red Hawk probably could not have caught him on foot.

Iron Knife, however, had no such intention.

Red Hawk had often thought of a battle with Iron Knife, and how it would end. He knew now that Iron Knife was a worthy foe. Red Hawk already had two knife nicks on his arm, while he had only drawn blood from Iron Knife once. Iron Knife had more experience in knife fights, that could be told from the number of scars he had on his arm. True knife fighters could be told by the scars on their arms.

Iron Knife ducked in and nicked Red Hawk again, which brought Red Hawk's mind back to business.

Iron Knife was surprised at Red Hawk's quickness. He had expected to be much quicker than the larger man, and that was not the case.

Red Hawk feinted in, slashed with his knife and opened another nick on Iron Knife's arm, which jerked the Nez Perce's mind back to the fray.

Ol' One-Eye was extremely interested in the outcome of the battle, and because of that began to creep forward to see better. At his age he relied more on his nose than on his one eye, and he had to get closer to see better.

He continued to edge closer and closer, until . . .

"Pike!"

At the sound of McConnell's voice Pike pulled his eyes from the two knife fighters and looked where McConnell was pointing.

There he was, Ol' One-Eye. He'd moved into plain sight and seemed to be watching the two Indians with great interest.

"Red Hawk! Iron Knife!" Pike called. "There is something you should see."

The Indians kept their eyes on one another, and then as if by silent consent, looked away from each other at Pike, and then beyond.

"It is him," Red Hawk said.

"The spirit wolf," Iron Knife said.

All four men were staring at the wolf, which just stood its ground and stared back haughtily.

Chapter Nineteen

"Are you reloaded?" Pike asked McConnell.

Sheepishly, McConnell admitted, "No. I started to, but—"

"Yes, I know," Pike said. "I got interested in the fight and didn't reload, either."

"So, what do we do now?" McConnell asked.

"All we have," Red Hawk said, "are our knives."

"None of you must approach him," Iron Knife said. "He is the Spirit Wolf."

"He is a wolf, and that is all," Red Hawk said. "There is no spirit within him."

"He *is* the Spirit Wolf," Iron Knife said, "and none of you will touch him."

Abruptly, Iron Knife put himself between them and the wolf, with his back to the animal. It was clear that if they wanted to approach the wolf, they were going to have to go through him.

"Reload," Pike said to McConnell, and proceeded to reload his pistol. The rifle he'd used was still on the ground near the other dead Nez Perce braves.

"No!" Iron Knife shouted. He rushed toward Pike and McConnell, but Red Hawk stepped between *them*. Iron Knife raised his knife, in defense of the "spirit wolf," but Red Hawk was quicker, and struck first. His knife penetrated Iron Knife's side, and glanced off a rib. Iron Knife backed away swiftly, and clasped a hand to his bleeding side. His other hand released his knife, which fell to the ground.

"Iron Knife—" Pike said, but the wounded Nez Perce brave abruptly turned and ran toward the one-eyed wolf.

"Away!" he shouted. "Away, spirit wolf, to safety—"

He was waving his free arm as he ran, trying to warn the wolf off, when suddenly the wolf sprang.

"Damn!" Pike said, hurriedly trying to reload now.

The wolf sprang true and his jaws closed on Iron Knife's throat. The Nez Perce went down beneath the wolf's weight, and the wolf took only a second to tear out his throat.

Pike, reloaded, raised his pistol. At the same moment Red Hawk seemed to remember his rifle and bent to pick it up, but the wolf was already running off. Pike started after him.

"Pike, wait!" McConnell shouted.

"If we don't get him now," Pike called back, "we may never get another chance."

"He is right," Red Hawk said. He started after Pike and McConnell, now also reloaded, brought up the rear.

"Spread out!" McConnell called ahead, and they all did just that.

Pike followed the wolf's path while Red Hawk and McConnell veered off to either side of him, hoping to surround the wolf.

Pike ran as fast as he could, the pistol held at shoulder height in his hand. He thought he could hear Ol' One-Eye pounding through the brush ahead of him, and then suddenly there was nothing.

He stopped and listened, but could hear nothing.

"Pike!" McConnell called from somewhere off to his left.

"I lost him!" Pike shouted back. "Red Hawk?"

From his right Red Hawk shouted, "I don't know where he is!"

"Damn it," Pike said beneath his breath. He continued forward, but the ground around him was hard and hadn't held the wolf's tracks. "Double damn."

Suddenly, McConnell appeared from his left, and Red Hawk from his right.

"Where the hell did he go?" Pike asked.

McConnell shrugged and Red Hawk was stolid.

"Damn it, he's not a spirit, right?" Pike said. "He can't have just disappeared."

"Let's go back to camp," McConnell said. "We can try and pick up his trail."

"The ground's hard—" Pike said, but stopped himself even before Red Hawk cut him off.

"There are other ways," the Snake brave said.

"Yeah," McConnell said, "I know, I know."

McConnell led the way back to camp, followed by Red Hawk. Pike stood behind several more seconds, staring about him, wondering where the hell the wolf could have disappeared to.

There hadn't even been a puff of smoke.

When they got back to the camp Iron Knife's body was gone.

"Shit," Pike said, staring down at where the body had been. It had not been dragged off for there were no telltale heel marks.

"Did anyone stop to check and make sure he was dead?" McConnell asked.

"I didn't."

"I did not," Red Hawk said.

167

"Neither did I," McConnell said.

"He had to be dead, damn it," Pike said. "The wolf took his throat out."

"That's the way it looked, all right," McConnell said. "What do you think? The wolf doubled back and took him?"

Pike looked at McConnell sharply, to see if his friend was making fun of him, but McConnell's expression appeared to be serious.

"That could not be," Red Hawk said, also treating the question seriously. "The animal would have dragged the body. We would see the marks."

The ground was hard, but it would have showed drag marks, and it did not.

"Then he got up and walked off," Pike said. "That's the only answer."

"I suggest we break camp and try to pick up the wolf's trail," McConnell said. "We've already wasted too much time with De Roche and the Nez Perce."

"Let's check the others first," Pike said, "and make sure they're dead."

McConnell and Red Hawk nodded, and while they checked the other Nez Perce to see if they were indeed dead, Pike went and checked on the ones he had disposed of. They were still where he left them, and very dead. He picked up the borrowed rifle and went back to join the others.

"My two are dead, and still there."

"These two are dead," McConnell said. "No question."

"All right, then," Pike said. "Let's break camp."

They set about doing just that, each quiet with his own thoughts. The disappearance of Iron Knife—or of Iron Knife's body—was still very much on their minds.

*   *   *

168

Ol' One-Eye reached his pack, which were becoming impatient. They were hungry. He gathered them together, then took the lead and started to show them to food.

He would take them to the only place he knew for sure there was food.

Mounted up, Pike, McConnell and Red Hawk rode back to where they had lost the one-eyed wolf. Red Hawk dismounted and started checking for sign.

He mounted up again and said, "This way."

Pike and McConnell let him take the lead without argument.

It was not long before Red Hawk called a halt to their progress and turned his horse to face them.

"He's going back."

"What?" Pike asked.

"He has rejoined the pack, and is leading them back the way we have come."

"Back to the Fort," McConnell said. "The damn pack must be hungry."

"And they'll find plenty of food back at the Fort," Pike said.

"My people are also in danger."

"We've got to get back, then," Pike said. "To hell with following the pack. We'll just have to head back and warn our people."

"Agreed," Red Hawk said.

"The size of the pack has to be reduced," Pike said. "If we can get to our people and alert them, we might be able to take care of them for good, this time."

"Can we join forces, Red Hawk?" McConnell asked.

"We have joined forces, my friend," Red Hawk said,

"but what do you think your people, and my people, would say to that?"

McConnell looked at Pike and said, "It might be a hard sell."

"We'd be too busy watching each other to fight the pack," Pike said.

"We will have to warn our own people, and take our chances," Red Hawk said.

"Let's get to it, then," Pike said. "Even stopping for the night, if we ride hard we can get back by tomorrow night."

Idly, he wondered who would get to the fort first, them or the doctor for young Barry.

If young Barry was in any condition to be helped by a doctor.

They rode back the way they had come, and when they reached their old campsite they saw that the wolves had been there. The bodies of the Indians had been ravaged.

"The pack must be starving," Red Hawk said. "They would not usually feed on human carcasses."

Pike checked on the other two Nez Perce and found them in the same condition.

Wordlessly, they left the cold campsite and continued on.

Ol' One-Eye had lost control of the pack when they crossed the campsite where the dead Indians were. He had to stand by and watch as the pack fed on the dead humans. Only when they were done was he able to regain control. They were far from sated, and eagerly followed their leader.

They had gone much farther when Red Hawk called them to a halt.

"What is it?" Pike asked.

"I thought I heard something."

They all sat quietly and soon they all heard it, a low moan.

"It sounds like a man," McConnell said.

"This way," Red Hawk said.

He turned his horse to the right and they followed. Before long they saw the body lying on the ground, and heard the moaning again.

"It can't be," McConnell said.

They dismounted and moved to the body. Red Hawk reached it first and turned it over.

It was Iron Knife.

"Jesus," McConnell said, "he's still alive."

The Nez Perce brave was covered with blood from his throat wound. It looked to them as if his entire throat had been torn out.

"How could he be alive?" Pike asked.

"What can we do for him?" McConnell asked.

"Nothing," Red Hawk said. He stood up and walked away from them.

"Pike," McConnell said, "we've got to do somethin' for him."

"Only one thing we can do, Skins," Pike said.

Pike pulled the Kentucky pistol from his belt, placed the barrel against the side of Iron Knife's head, and pulled the trigger.

When they walked back to the horses Red Hawk was sitting his pony stiffly. He did not say a word to them as they remounted.

Secretly, Pike was relieved. Iron Knife had been

alive and had walked off on his own. He'd walked as far as he could go, and then had fallen where they found him. No "spirit wolf" had come along and whisked him away.

As they started their journey again, Pike suddenly wondered how the man had walked as far as he had without leaving a trail of blood.

Chapter Twenty

It was still light enough for De Roche to see them. He had not moved from his camp on the ridge. His instincts told him that the wolves would be back, and there they were.

As he looked down at them he saw the gray back of Ol' One-Eye as he led the pack past the ridge. De Roche counted as they went by, and saw that the pack's number was down to nine.

If he'd had his rifle he would have been able to pick Ol' One-Eye off right from there. The wolf was out of range of his pistol. With their leader dead, the pack would have either scattered, or gone off to wait for a new leader to take his place. He owed this lost opportunity to McConnell, and also to Pike. Mostly, however, it was McConnell, because he was the one who had gotten the drop on him and left him here. He'd pay them both back.

Right now, however, he had to get on the pack's trail. He threw all of his supplies aside and mounted the mule. All he took with him was some dried beef, a canteen, and his pistol.

Somewhere behind him, he knew, were Pike, McConnell and Red Hawk, but Ol' One-Eye came first, because the wolf was worth money.

Vengeance would have to come later.

It was almost dark when they reached the site of their old camp. McConnell had ridden ahead to check on De Roche, and see if he was still around.

When McConnell came upon De Roche's campsite he saw that the Frenchman had left most of his supplies behind. When he put his hand over the extinguished campfire he could still feel some heat. Had De Roche sat here all this time, just waiting for them to come back? Why not? He was the wolf hunter, and had apparently correctly predicted that the wolves would come back this way.

McConnell wheeled his horse to ride down and tell Pike and Red Hawk what he had found.

"Camping here again," Pike said, "it's as if we've made no progress."

"But we have," Red Hawk said. "We no longer have to worry about the Nez Perce, and we have had another encounter with the wolf."

Pike noticed that when Red Hawk called Ol' One-Eye "the" wolf, it was as if the word THE was capitalized.

"I expect De Roche will be long gone," Pike said. "Maybe he's even back at Fort Hall by now."

"If he did go back to the fort, he is probably back on the trail, by now. If he is lucky he will run into the pack."

"Or if he's unlucky," Pike added.

They had a fire built by the time McConnell returned from his scouting.

"From the way it looks," McConnell said, "De Roche was up there until a little while ago. The ashes

174

in his fire are still warm."

Pike looked up at the ridge and said, "He knew."

"That's what I figure," McConnell said.

"Knew what?" Red Hawk asked.

"He knew that we'd be back this way," Pike said. "He knew the wolves would be back this way."

"How did he know that?"

"He's got something on his side that we don't," Pike said. "He hunts wolves for a living."

"We have all hunted," Red Hawk said, as if he were reluctant to admit that De Roche had an edge on him.

"Yes, we've all hunted," Pike said, "but he hunts *wolves*. Whether we like it or not, that gives him the edge over us."

"What's the difference?" McConnell asked.

Both Pike and Red Hawk looked at him.

"I mean, what does it matter if De Roche is the one who kills Ol' One-Eye. The beast will be just as dead. Come on, fellas, let's not keep making this personal."

"It's personal for you, too, Skins," Pike said.

"How do you mean?"

"De Roche," Pike said. "He's going to hold it against all of us that we disarmed him and left him behind, but he's got to hold it against you the most. You're the one who got the drop on him. You're the one who humiliated him."

"If he gets his wolf," McConnell said, "all he's gonna care about is gettin' his money."

"And after that?" Pike asked.

McConnell thought a moment, then said, "Jesus, what other good news can you come up with?"

"Just one thing," Pike said.

"What's that?"

"De Roche is on a mule, so we'll probably be able to catch up to him."

"Unless he rides through the night," Red Hawk pointed out.

"That's right," McConnell said. "Mules are sure-footed, and he might decide to do just that."

"Well, I'm not riding through the night," Pike said. "We'll get an early start in the morning. At least that way none of us will end up with a horse with a broken leg."

McConnell did not point out that he had ridden through the night to catch up with them.

"I wonder," he said.

"Wonder what?"

"Whether or not the wolves will travel during the night?"

"I don't know," Pike said, and looked at Red Hawk.

"I do not know, either."

De Roche decided to stop for the night. He built a fire and dined on dried beef and water from his canteen. He was in no hurry. He knew where the pack was headed, and he'd get there soon enough.

He wondered how the citizens of Fort Hall would react when the wolves arrived. He had seen wolves cause so much panic that a small number of them was able to clear an entire settlement. Here were nine wolves, led by a creature who struck fear into the heart of anyone who had ever heard of him, or seen him.

He just hoped that Locke made it out alive, because he wanted to be able to collect the second half of his money. After that, after he was paid, then he'd go after McConnell, and Pike . . . and hell yes, maybe even Red Hawk. Why not do away with all his enemies all at once?

*   *   *

176

Ol' One-Eye forced the pack to stop for the night. He knew they were hungry, but this was his way of flaunting his dominance over them.

Soon, he assured them, soon you will feed.

There was a chill in the air—more of a chill than usual. Everyone at Fort Hall felt it.

Locke wondered what was happening out there. With Pike, McConnell, De Roche, Ol' One-Eye and his wolves, there was the potential for a very explosive situation. He hated to think it, but as long as Ol' One-Eye didn't make it out alive Fort Hall would benefit.

Idly, though, he wondered which of the men would come back, and which would be left out there to rot.

Jean Windham was past the point where she was worried about the man called Jack Pike. All she thought about now was the damned doctor, and when he would get here. When she was in the room with her son she could *smell* the infection in the air. Barry was still holding on, but how much longer could he do so without medical attention?

And when the doctor did finally arrive, would he be able to do anything, or would the infection have spread too far by then?

That damned wolf, she thought, tears rolling down her face as she sat by her son's bedside. First he took her husband, and he might take her son.

She looked over at the corner of the tent, where she had taken to keeping her husband's rifle. If that wolf came back, with or without his pack, he was not going to leave Fort Hall alive.

That she swore.

177

*   *   *

Barry Windham, in his delirium, kept having the same dream over and over again. The wolf was savaging his father, and Pike was there, poised to fire his rifle, but before he could fire the dream would just start all over again. It never ended, and even in his deep sleep Barry knew it would never end until Ol' One-Eye was dead.

Only then would he wake up.

Red Hawk took the first watch, would wake McConnell in three hours, and then Pike would finish it up.

Pike lay inside his blanket and thought about the boy, Barry. Without a doctor the chances were good that the boy was dead by now. Even if Pike—or Red Hawk, or even De Roche—managed to kill the wolf, what good would that do Jean Windham? Sure, she'd have revenge for the deaths of her son and husband, but what would she do after that? Would the hide of the beast who murdered her family be any consolation to her?

He was forced to agree with McConnell. At this point it did not matter to him who killed the wolf, as long as it was killed. He had to get on with his life, and so would Jean Windham.

Much the same thoughts were running through Red Hawk's head as he stood watch. What really mattered was that "the" wolf died, not who killed him. He wanted to get back to his wife, and back to his life. It was time for both he and Pike to come to their senses

178

and realize this. Silently, Red Hawk gave thanks for Skins McConnell, and his refusal to become personally involved in the hunt for "the" wolf.

Why he was keeping watch he didn't know. The dangers were all ahead of them, now.

He hoped.

Chapter Twenty-One

In the morning all the players in the hunt woke early and got under way . . .

Ol' One-Eye was awake and alert even before the sun came up, and was not gentle in waking the pack. It was just another way in which he reminded them who the leader was. As the sun was coming up, they were padding their way to Fort Hall . . .

De Roche was up with the sun. It was as if its touch on his skin was like a hand, waking him. He doused his fire and breakfasted on dried beef and water while astride the mule. He caressed the Kentucky pistol in his belt. McConnell had been soft enough of heart—and head—to leave it with him, and it would be his undoing.

Pike woke Red Hawk and McConnell before the sun, but by the time they were ready to move, part of the big orange ball was showing above a mountain peak.

"I get the feeling we're all up early today," he said to the others.

"I have that same feeling," McConnell said.

"Today," Red Hawk said, "it will all end today."

Jean Windham stuck her head out of the tent just long enough to determine that the sun was coming up, and to take a breath of fresh air. The air inside was now fetid with the stink of her son's infection.

Could even a doctor save him now?

Andrew Locke was opening up his business with the sun. He had a feeling that today someone would be coming for the rest of that money. He still believed that if Pike and McConnell killed the wolf they would accept the money. Why else would anyone go after a wolf like Ol' One-Eye?

They'd have to be crazy not to be doing it for the money.

"Look," Red Hawk said, pointing at the ground.

"I see it," Pike said. "So."

"The tracks of the pack, and the tracks of the mule De Roche is riding," Red Hawk said.

"I said I see it," Pike said. "What are you getting at?"

"Getting at?"

"What's your point?" McConnell asked.

"De Roche is following the pack."

Pike stared at Red Hawk as if the Snake brave had lost his mind.

182

"We can see that."

"We do not have to follow the pack," Red Hawk said.

"What do you mean?"

"We can go that way," Red Hawk said, pointing, "and get to the Fort first."

"It's a short cut?" Pike asked.

"If that is what you call it."

"Wait a minute," McConnell said, and Red Hawk looked at him. "If we go that way, you'll be bypassing your camp."

"If you go that way," Red Hawk said, "I will continue this way. We will each warn our own people."

"Split up, you mean," McConnell said.

"Yes," Red Hawk said, "split up."

McConnell looked at Pike and said, "I'm game. Let's get movin'."

Pike looked at Red Hawk and extended his hand.

"Good luck to you and your people."

Red Hawk hesitated a moment, then took Pike's hand.

"And to you," he said. "The first one to see the wolf kills it. Agreed?"

Pike squeezed Red Hawk's hand and said, "Agreed."

Red Hawk released Pike's hand and nodded to McConnell, then started his horse and continued to follow the tracks on the ground.

"What about De Roche?" McConnell asked.

"What about him?" Pike said.

"Does the same go for him?" McConnell asked. "First one to see him kills him?"

Pike didn't answer.

"We'd better get moving, straight that way."

They started off, and about twenty minutes later they saw the cloud.

"What the hell is that?" McConnell asked.

"A black cloud," Pike said, "and it looks like it's right over Fort Hall."

They rode in silence for a few moments and then McConnell said, "You know, I think you may be right."

"About what?"

"About Ol' One-Eye being some kind of spirit wolf."

"I didn't call him a spirit wolf," Pike said, "the Nez Perce did."

"Well, you think he's somethin' more than just a wolf, and I'm sayin' now that you may be right."

"You think the wolf is the cause of the black cloud?" Pike asked.

"I don't know."

"It's just a storm cloud, Skins."

"Sure."

"Let's stop talking nonsense and get to the Fort."

"I'm with you."

A wolf is just a wolf, Pike told himself.

Just a wolf.

When the two riders appeared Jean Windham squinted in an attempt to see better. Neither of the riders was large enough to be Pike, and then she recognized one of them as the rider who had been sent for the doctor.

"Doctor," she said, and then she shouted, "Doctor!" and started to run.

When Pike and McConnell reached Fort Hall it was quiet. Pike looked over at the tent where Barry Windham was being kept. There were several people outside, one of whom was Andrew Locke. He and McConnell rode over.

Locke looked up and saw them as they approached. He broke away from the others and walked toward them.

"Where is it?" he asked.

"Where is what?" Pike asked.

"The wolf," Locke said, "Ol' One-Eye. Where is it?"

"Oh," Pike said, "he'll be along."

Locke frowned.

"Did De Roche get it?"

"No."

Locke looked even more puzzled.

"You didn't get it, and De Roche didn't get it. How is it coming?"

"How's the boy?"

"The doctor's in with him now."

"I'll take the horses," McConnell said.

Pike nodded, dismounted and handed his horse over to his friend.

"Meet me at Locke's."

"Right."

He started for the tent and stopped when Locke put his hand on his arm.

"Where's the wolf, Pike?"

"Get your people together at your place, Locke," Pike said. "The wolf is on his way here with the pack."

"What? But . . . but you were supposed to kill it. I don't understand."

"Now we can all kill it," Pike said. "You'd better talk to your people and get them ready. We don't have much time."

He left Locke standing there and went to the tent. He didn't know any of the people standing outside, so he walked past them and entered the tent.

185

Barry was lying where Pike had left him. On one side of the bed was Jean, and on the other side was a man who was obviously a doctor. Pike remained silent and stood there while the doctor continued to examine the boy.

At one point Jean seemed to sense that Pike was there. She looked up at him and he was shocked at how haggard she looked. She motioned for him to stay there, got up and walked over to him.

"Did you get it?" she asked. "Did you get the wolf that did this to my little boy?"

"Not yet," Pike said, "but we will. How is Barry doing?"

"The doctor says his wounds are terribly infected. He's going to try and clean them, and then wrap them up. After that he says it's up to Barry."

"He's a strong kid."

"The doctor says that his youth is in his favor. Pike, I don't understand. What happened with the wolf?"

"Jean, the wolf is on his way back here, with his pack."

"Oh, my God."

"We're going to be ready for them," Pike said. "We'll finish them all."

"Pike—"

"You just worry about Barry," Pike said. "I have to go and talk to Locke and the people of the settlement."

"Will you be staying here?"

"I'll be here until the wolf is dead, Jean."

She nodded, then hurried back to her son's side.

Pike stepped outside and stopped among the people there.

"Any of you people own rifles?"

Several of them nodded, and a couple of women said that their husbands did.

"Get your rifles, or your husbands, and meet over at Andrew Locke's place."

"What's going on?" a man asked.

"We'll meet over there," Pike said, "and I'll tell you all about it."

"Wait a minute," another man said. "Who are you?"

Pike stared at the man and said, "I'm the man who just gave you your instructions, friend. If you want this settlement to survive, I suggest you follow them."

Chapter Twenty-Two

Pike met McConnell and Locke at Locke's Trading Post, and together the three of them waited for the people of the settlement to arrive.

"They're not gonna like this, you know," Locke said.

"Why not?" McConnell asked.

"They all put up money to hire someone to kill the wolf," Locke explained. "They never expected to have to do it themselves."

"Well, maybe they should have expected it."

"Where's De Roche? Maybe he's killed the wolf already. Maybe he'll bring it in."

"I hope he has killed it," Pike said. "I really do, but I doubt it."

"I think De Roche will be along soon," McConnell said. "We had a, er, run-in with him along the way, and had to take his rifle away from him."

"What? How's he supposed to kill the thing without his rifle?"

"Well, I caught him pointing the thing the wrong way, and was forced to take it from him."

"He's not gonna like that," Locke said "I'd be careful around De Roche if I was you."

"So I've been told."

"Let's forget about all of that now, Locke," Pike said. "We've got other things to be concerned about."

"Just as long as nobody expects me to go out there with a rifle."

Pike turned to face Locke.

"As booshway," he said, "you're the first one I expect to be out there with a rifle."

"What?"

The room was filling up slowly, people trying to find a place to sit. There were so few of those that before long there were more people standing than sitting. There were a few women there, but they were far outnumbered by the men. The last person to walk into the room was Jean Windham, and Pike noticed that she was carrying a rifle. He recognized the rifle as the one young Barry was holding when he was attacked by the wolf. He was going to have to pull her aside when he was finished talking to the crowd.

"I think we can get started now," Pike said.

"Wait a minute," Locke said. "What are you gonna tell them?"

McConnell clapped Locke on the shoulder and said, "Listen like everyone else."

"Can I have your attention please?" Pike called out.

The same man who had asked Pike who he was spoke up again, but this time he was talking to Locke.

"Andy, who is this fella? Why should we be listening to him?"

Pike looked at Locke expectantly.

"Uh, Joe, everyone, this is Jack Pike and Skins McConnell. They've just come back from tryin' to hunt down the wolf that injured young Barry Windham."

"Ol' One-Eye?" the man called Joe said. "Did they get 'im?"

"No," Locke said, "but if you'll all listen to Pike, he's

190

gonna tell you how to finally kill the beast." Mentally, Locke added, I hope.

"How we can kill the beast?" someone asked.

"That's right," Pike said. "The fact of the matter is we trailed the wolf and he and his pack are on the way back here."

"Back here? Why?" another voice asked. It was a woman, and it was apparent in her tone that she was frightened. Pike couldn't blame her.

"This is their best source of food in the area," Pike said.

"Food?" another woman said. "You mean us?"

"I mean your livestock. Wolf packs rarely attack men—and women—for food."

"What about Barry Windham?" the man called Joe demanded. "He got attacked."

"That was an isolated incident," Pike said.

"The way I heard it," a man in the back said, "you and your partner were attacked, also."

"No," Pike said, "our camp was attacked, and the wolves went after our livestock. They didn't go after us at all."

"That's no guarantee they won't go after some people when they get here," someone said.

"If they get here," Joe said, "we only have Pike's word for that. Besides, where's De Roche, the wolf hunter we hired?"

The crowd took up the cry of "where's De Roche" and Locke had to step forward again.

"De Roche has not returned," Locke said. "He's either still out there hunting the beast, or . . ."

"Or what?" somebody asked.

"Or he's dead, that's what," another said. "Whataya think?"

"Look," Pike shouted, "this is getting us nowhere.

We all have to get ready for the arrival of the pack."

"Why us?" a woman said. "We hired De Roche for that. We have you for that."

"I'm not for hire, Ma'am," Pike said. "I want this wolf dead simply to safeguard this settlement, and I don't even live here. I would think that those of you who live here would want to safeguard it, too . . . if only for your children."

The people started arguing among themselves. Some of them agreed with Pike, but most of them felt that they should hire someone else, if necessary.

"Listen to me, listen to me," Pike called out. "Those of you who have rifles, get them. We're not only talking about one wolf, here, we're talking about a pack of wolves—but the pack has been thinned out. If we have enough guns, we can take care of them."

"You can take care of them," the man called Joe said. He started for the door and said, "I have a wife and kid to worry about, and I'm staying with them. I advise you all to go to your homes."

"No," Pike said, "you'll do no good hiding in your homes."

For the most part, he was unheeded as people surged for the doorway. By the time those who wanted to leave were gone there were about six men left in the room, and one woman—Jean Windham.

"I assume you men are willing to work with me?" Pike asked.

They exchanged glances and without a word seemed to choose a spokesman.

"We want to save this settlement, Pike," a man named Kevin Mack said. "This is our home and we're not givin' up to no wolves."

"Do we know how many there are?" another man asked.

192

"Near as we can figure," Pike said, "as few as nine, as many as fifteen."

"And they're led by Ol' One-Eye?"

"That's right."

Pike looked around, examining the faces of the men who had stayed. They looked anything but sure of themselves. In fact, the only face in the room that reflected any kind of determination was Jean Windham's.

"All right," Pike said, "tell my partner here your names, and then go and get your rifles and come back."

"Tonight?" Mack asked.

"There's nothing that says the pack won't attack at night," Pike said. "I don't really think they will, but I want to start working on a strategy with all of you."

Mack nodded, and the men started to file out. Jean Windham, who had been leaning against the wall, pushed away, picked up her rifle and approached Pike.

"I already have my rifle."

Pike took hold of Jean's arm, turned to Locke and said, "Bring me a beer, will you, Locke?" To Jean he said, "Come over here with me," and led her to a table.

They sat down at a small table and Pike took the rifle from her.

"Do you know how to fire this?"

"Of course."

"Do you know how to load it."

"I—isn't it loaded?"

"Yes, it's loaded," Pike said, "but what are you going to do after you fire this shot?"

Jean stared at him defiantly.

"Maybe I wouldn't miss with the first shot."

"Don't be a fool, Jean," he said. "Almost everyone misses on the first shot. You've got to be able to load fast enough to get a second."

"Then teach me how to load."

"Sure, I'll teach you," Pike said, "after we take care of the wolf."

"I want a shot at him, Pike," she said, fervently.

"Not with this," he said, handing the rifle back.

"Why not?"

"Jean, if either you or Barry had fired this it would have blown up in your face." He was exaggerating, but the rifle was way too dirty to ever be fired without a complete cleaning.

She stared at the rifle as if it had just betrayed her.

"Then you loan me a rifle," she said, finally.

"I can't," he said, laughing ironically. "My rifle's been damaged and I have to borrow one. Right now I've got De Roche's, and he's going to want it back when he gets here."

"Then what am I supposed to do?"

Pike leaned toward her as Locke came over and set a beer down in front of him. He waited for Locke to leave before speaking.

"Stay with your son, Jean," Pike said. "Hold his hand, talk to him so he knows that you're there. While you're there you might say a prayer for him as well . . . and for the rest of us."

She stared at Pike, and then tears started streaming down from her eyes. Awkwardly, he reached over and covered her hands with his. Her hands were stiff, the skin dry. They were work-roughened hands.

"All right," she said, finally, "all right. I'll stay with him if you'll promise me one thing."

"What's that?"

"You won't let it get away this time," she said. Her hands came up and grabbed his in an iron grip. "Promise me!"

He hesitated, and then said, "All right, Jean. I promise."

194

As she left he hoped he wouldn't be sorry.

Skins McConnell came walking over with a beer in his hand and sat down.

"What was that about?"

"She wanted to volunteer."

"You told her no?"

"We don't need a woman with a badly rusted gun, Skins. She might shoot herself in the foot, or shoot somebody else by mistake."

"What did you promise her?"

Pike hesitated, then said, "That we'd kill Ol' One-Eye, this time."

"And what if we don't?"

Pike looked at McConnell and said, "We will. This time we will."

"With these men?" McConnell asked. "If one of them can shoot, we'll be lucky. If any of them know how to hold a rifle we'll be lucky."

"Let's wait and find out before we run them down, Skins."

"Sure," McConnell said, "we'll wait."

"Did you tell those fellas to come right back here?" Pike asked.

"I did," McConnell said. "They'll probably be here by the time we finish these beers."

Idly, Pike said, "I wonder when De Roche will get here?"

"If we're lucky," McConnell said, "he'll ride in on his mule with Ol' One-Eye's hide."

Pike looked at McConnell and said, "Could we get that lucky?"

Chapter Twenty-Three

When the six men returned with their rifles McConnell checked all of the weapons while Pike talked to the men. Locke's donation to the cause was beer for everyone—for free. He also supplied his rifle for inspection.

"Jesus," one of the men said, "for free beer I'd hunt bears naked."

"What's your name?" Pike asked.

"Ozzie Whitehurst."

Whitehurst looked as if drinking beer was what he did best. He was a good thirty pounds overweight, most of it in the belly, and at five ten or less he was not tall enough to carry it.

"Can you shoot?"

"I can load and fire," Whitehurst said. "I don't know as I'd say I can shoot."

"What about the rest of you?" Pike said aloud. "Who can shoot?"

Two hand went up tentatively, and then a third.

"You either can, or you can't," Pike said to the owner of the third hand, who quickly put his hand down.

Of the two men who raised their hands, one was Kevin Mack.

"What's your name?" Pike asked the other man.

"Willie McGee."

"Mr. McGee—"

"Just Willie," McGee said. He was a young man in his early twenties, tall but slightly built. Like as not he'd put on weight as he got older.

"Willie," Pike said, "can you hit what you shoot at?"

"More often than not."

"Mack?"

"The same?"

"On the move?"

"I've hunted some," McGee said.

"Hunted what?"

"Small game."

"Mack?"

"Some small game, some deer."

"All right," Pike said, "listen up."

The five men lifted their heads, and McConnell had just finished checking their weapons when the door opened and De Roche stepped in.

Andrew Locke stared at De Roche from behind the bar. De Roche walked right to the bar and said, "Beer."

Locke put a beer in front of the Frenchman and asked, "Did you get it?"

"Get what?" De Roche asked.

"The wolf," Locke said. "Did you get it?"

"Didn't they tell you?" De Roche asked.

"Tell me what?"

De Roche ignored Locke.

"They, uh, told me you had a run-in."

"A run-in," De Roche said, laughing. "They left me out there with a mule and a pistol, so they could kill the wolf first and collect my money."

"They didn't kill it," Locke said. "It's still out there. They say that the whole pack is headed this way."

De Roche looked at Locke and said, "They are probably right."

"De Roche," Pike said.

The Frenchman turned and looked at Pike.

"You have my rifle," De Roche said.

"Skins," Pike said, "give him his rifle."

McConnell picked up the rifle, walked to the bar and handed it to De Roche.

"Merci," De Roche said, taking it. "You and I, *mon ami,* we have ze unfinished business."

"We all have unfinished business, De Roche," Pike said, "with a wolf."

"That is true, Pike," De Roche said, "we do—but afterward, our business will be concluded, eh?"

"You followed the trail of the pack, De Roche," Pike said, "What happened?"

"The trail . . . ended."

"What do you mean, it ended?" Pike asked.

"Just what I said," De Roche said. "It just ended. Poof! Gone."

"How could that be?" Pike asked.

"Perhaps, as the Nez Perce say, ze wolf is a devil wolf, eh? A spirit wolf?"

"What?" Locke said.

"So, with no trail to follow, I came here," De Roche said. "I must agree with you, Pike. The pack is coming here."

"If you kill it, De Roche, you still get the money?"

De Roche looked at Locke, nodded, and then looked around the room.

"Is this your army, Pike? Are these the men you are going to use against the pack?"

"Do you have a better idea, De Roche?"

"Hunting a wolf is not a game for amateurs, my friends," De Roche said to the other men.

"We'll take our chances, De Roche," Pike said, quickly, before anyone else could speak. "Of course, if you helped we'd have an even better chance."

"Ah, you would like to join forces, eh? What happened to your other partner, eh? Red Hawk?"

"Red Hawk?" Locke said. "Who's that?"

"Never mind, Locke," Pike said. "What do you say, De Roche? Will you help us?"

"You forget, my friend," De Roche said. "I hunt the wolf for money."

"I don't care who kills him," Pike said. "You can have your money no matter who kills him. What do you say, Locke?"

"What? Pay him even if he doesn't kill it?"

"Locke!"

Locke made a face and said, "Well, I—uh, sure, why not. As long as it's dead, right?"

"De Roche?"

"Under your leadership?" De Roche said.

"You want to be the leader?" Pike said. "Be my guest. You have the experience."

De Roche started to laugh.

"Ah, now you need me, eh? You would like to forget what happened out there? How you left me without a horse, without a rifle? I had a chance to kill the wolf, you know, but I did not have my rifle."

"I'm sorry about that, De Roche, but you weren't exactly pointing your rifle in the right direction, were you?" McConnell said.

De Roche finished his beer and put the empty mug down on the bar.

"I am sorry," De Roche said, "but I hunt alone."

With that he picked up his rifle.

"De Roche!" McConnell called.

The Frenchman turned and looked at him.

"I left your horse with Abel."

De Roche nodded, and left.

"We would have had a better chance with him, right?" Kevin Mack asked. "I mean, like you said, he's the expert, you said so yourself."

"Sure, we'd have been better off with him," Pike said, "but we'll just go ahead and do it without him. I want you men all to listen to me very closely."

After Pike had given the men their instructions he sent them outside, some to go home, some to stand watch. They all had their watch times, and would be relieving each other during the course of the night.

"Where will you be while we're standing watch?" one of the men asked.

"McConnell and I will be up all night, and one of us will always be here, and the other will always be outside, with you."

That seemed to satisfy the man, so they all picked up their rifles and went out.

"Locke."

"Yeah?" Locke said from behind the bar.

"I'll need a key to this place."

"A key," Locke said. "Uh, sure." He dug out a key and extended it over the bar. Pike walked over and took it. "What do you need a key for?"

"To get in and out," Pike said.

"But I'm here."

"No," Pike said, handing Locke his rifle, "you're outside."

"Wha—"

"And don't come back in for a couple of hours."

"But, my business—"

"Don't worry about your business," Pike said. "It'll still be here after we get rid of those wolves."

Frowning, Locke pulled on his coat and picked up

201

his rifle. He was grumbling as he went out the door.

"Who goes out first, you or me?" McConnell asked.

Pike took out a coin and said, "Call it."

"Heads."

Pike flipped it, let it fall to the table and slapped his palm over it. When he removed his hand the coin showed tails.

"That figures," McConnell said.

Chapter Twenty-Four

After a couple of hours McConnell came in and Pike went out. By now it was nightfall, with only a sliver of a moon for light. If the wolves chose this night to attack, they'd be damned hard to see, and even harder to shoot at and hit.

Pike checked to make sure that the men who were supposed to be outside were. He had to tell himself not to be so hard on them, because they were all there voluntarily. If they wanted to, they could tell him to go to hell, and go to their homes.

McConnell had not reported seeing De Roche, and Pike didn't see him during his two hours.

He wondered where the Frenchman was.

De Roche was lying on his back in a bed, with a whore on top of him. His thick penis was buried inside of her, and his hands were on her hips as she rode him up and down. She was a big woman with large breasts and fleshy hips. She had long dark hair that fell in front of her face when she leaned forward, and then away from her face when she threw her head back. He had been with this whore for three hours, because he had been out on the hunt for a long time. Even before he left the settlement to hunt Ol' One-Eye he hadn't had a chance to visit Miss Rachel's, so this was his first visit, and he wanted to make the most of it.

After she fell off him and lay beside him he grabbed one of her big breasts and pinched it.

"Ow, Jesus, whataya doin'?" she cried out.

"Go and get me another woman," he said.

"Hey, Mister, I don't work two girls to a man—"

"Then don't come back," he told her, "just send the other woman—and make it a blonde woman, this time."

"You wanna do it again, Mister? That's no problem—"

"I do want to do it again," he said, "but not with you. I want a blonde woman this time. Understand?"

"Sure," the dark-haired whore said, "I understand. You want a blonde, I'll get you a blonde."

She walked to the blanket that separated this "room" from the rest of the tent, her butt twitching, but when she reached it she turned around and said, "But you'll be wanting me back, you wait and see if you don't."

While he was waiting for the other woman he thought about Pike and his little army of wolf hunters. He laughed to himself. His instincts told him that Ol' One-Eye would not be bringing his pack in tonight, but if the pack did come he doubted that Pike's army would be able to stop them.

Tomorrow, he thought, they'll come tomorrow and he would ignore the pack. He would concentrate only on the leader, and after he had killed the one-eyed wolf and collected his money, Pike and McConnell would be next.

The blanket was pushed aside again and a naked blonde woman entered. She was as tall as the dark-

204

haired woman but this one had small breasts, like peaches, and hardly any hips at all.

"Come . . ." he said, holding out a hairy arm, one huge hand reaching for her . . .

During Pike's second shift inside the trading post the front door opened and he looked up to see who it was. He was surprised to see that it was Maria, the girl with the scar from the whorehouse—or whore "tent."

"Hello, Maria."

She closed the door and came into the room, approaching the table he was sitting at. He'd forgotten how small she was, but he hadn't forgotten how good she had been in bed that night. She had one hand up to her face, as if to hide the scar. He suspected it was something she did without really noticing it.

"I heard you were back," she said. "I hope you're . . . all right."

"Oh, I'm all right," Pike said. "Can I get you something to drink?"

"No, thank you."

"Aren't you supposed to be working?"

"I suppose," she said.

She had something on her mind, and he decided to let her get to it in her own time.

"When you left, I thought you'd never come back."

He grinned and said, "Well, I hope I didn't disappoint you too much."

"No," she said, seriously, "I'm not disappointed at all."

"Glad to hear it."

She came closer, so that she was standing right next to him.

"Maria, do you want to sit—"

205

"No," she said, cutting him off. She reached out and touched his face. "I want to make love with you."

"Maria," Pike said, "maybe tomorrow I can—"

"No," she said, her voice becoming breathy as her breathing quickened, "I mean now."

She put her hands out to cup his face, and he did not resist.

"When we made love," she said, "you made me feel like I was a real woman. You made me forget . . . this." She put her hand to her face where the scar was.

"Maria, go back—"

"I want you . . . here," she said. She tipped his face up and kissed him, her hot tongue invading his mouth. In spite of himself he began to react. She leaned over, continuing the kiss, and rubbing her hands along his thighs urgently.

"Maria," he said, pulling his mouth free, "not here . . ."

"Yes, here," she said, her tone raspy, "now . . ."

Her hands avidly unbuttoned his pants and he found himself lifting his hips to help her pull them down. He looked at the door nervously, finding himself more excited than he had been in some time. The fact that anyone could walk in at any time seemed to increase the excitement.

He felt her hands on his underwear, yanking them down, and then his erection was jutting from his lap. She swooped down on it, first with her hands and then with her mouth, hotly devouring him.

"God . . ." he said, cupping her head as she began to ride him up and down. He reached underneath to unbutton her shirt, and her small, hard breasts blossomed into his hands. Her nipples were extremely hard, and her flesh was burning hot.

She released him from her mouth, and stood to remove her pants. He slid his hands beneath her firm

206

buttocks and lifted her onto his lap. She caught her breath as he penetrated her, and wiggled down onto his lap until he was totally buried inside of her.

"Oh, Jesus . . ." she moaned, moving on him. He still had hold of her buttocks and began to lift her up and down on him. She wrapped her arms around his neck and he leaned forward to kiss and suck on her breasts. At that moment, anyone could have entered the room and neither of them would have noticed.

In the quiet room the sound of their breathing was almost explosive. As he felt the rush building in his legs he had the urge to stand up, and gave into it. He stood, his hands on her ass taking her weight, and she continued to move against him, her arms around his neck, squirming against him as he turned and started to walk across the room. He could feel her wetness on his hands.

"Oh," Maria screamed, clinging to him, "Oh Pike, yes . . ."

He slid his hands from her ass to the underside of her thighs, which were slick with perspiration, and lifted her higher as they reached the bar. They banged into it, almost upsetting it, and then he braced his legs as he exploded inside of her and she shouted out loud, her nails digging into the back of his neck.

He wrapped his arms around her and held her tightly, and then slowly lowered her to the floor. Her legs refused to hold her for a moment, and he held her to keep her from sinking to the floor.

"Jesus," he said, then, "anybody could walk in here . . ."

He walked across the room to retrieve their pants. He tossed hers to her while he tried to pull his own on over his boots. He didn't even remember how she had managed to get his pants off with his boots still on, but apparently she had been eager enough to do it.

His pants were back on, as were hers, and she was buttoning her shirt when the door opened and Skins McConnell walked in. A couple of minutes earlier and Pike might have had some explaining to do.

"Um," McConnell said, "excuse me, am I interrupting something."

"No," Pike said, truthfully, "no, we were just . . . getting reacquainted."

"Will I see you tomorrow?" Maria asked. She looked as if she were fighting a smile.

"Yes," Pike said, "tomorrow." Maybe, he thought. Tomorrow she would show him a real smile.

As she walked past McConnell and out of the room Pike realized that he could still smell her. Watching McConnell, he knew that his friend could also smell the combined scent of sweat and sex.

"I think it's your turn to go outside," McConnell said.

"Right," Pike said.

As Pike walked past McConnell his friend said, "You still got the key?"

"Sure," Pike said, "you want it?"

"No," McConnell said, "you might need it, next time . . . you know?"

His friend was telling him that next time he should lock the door.

"Right," Pike said, "next time."

Outside Pike stopped and took a deep breath. His own perspiration beneath his clothes had dried, and he felt the need for a bath. Maybe later, he would go and take it with Maria . . .

He walked toward the tent where Jean and Barry Windham were, wondering if she was awake. He stuck his head inside and saw that she was seated by her son's

208

bedside, her head down. He decided not to disturb her. She needed all the rest she could get.

He checked on the position of the men. Since they had six men to work with, Pike had constructed a schedule of two men on watch at a time, plus himself and McConnell. He placed one man at the north end of the settlement, and one at the south. As he walked to the south end to check with Kevin Mack he realized that there was some unmined manpower. The men he did have were men who lived in the settlement, but there were also men staying in Dominick Abel's small tent camp, some of them merely staying for the night. Others, however, might have been staying longer, and might even be willing to help out in the crisis.

He decided that when the sun came up he would go and check with those men, and see how many were willing to assist. Surely, among them he'd find men who were accustomed to using a weapon.

When De Roche finished with the blonde he decided to go and find his own girl, this time. He left his blanketed "room" and proceeded to wander the tent, naked. His manhood was still hard, jutting in front of him. His front and back was covered with hair, and his short legs were corded with muscles.

"Hey, Mister—" Miss Rachel said when she saw him. "Hey, you can't walk around like that."

"I need another woman," De Roche said.

"Hey, you pay, you can have all the women you want, but I'll send them to you—"

"I want to pick one out myself."

She stared at De Roche, wondering if he was drunk. He acted drunk, but she supplied no liquor in her place, and he hadn't brought any with him.

She stared at his rigid manhood for a moment,

209

wondering if she should come out of retirement just this once, when abruptly he looked past her.

"I want her!" he said.

She turned and saw that Maria had just entered the tent.

"Oh, she's not one of the girls," Miss Rachel said. "Besides, she got a scar—"

"I don't care," De Roche said. "I want her."

"Mister, I got plenty of girls—"

"I'll pay double."

Miss Rachel stopped, took only a moment to decide, then turned and called out, "Maria . . ."

Chapter Twenty-Five

"What about sleep?" McConnell asked.

"What?"

"See," McConnell said to Pike, "you need some sleep, too."

"Oh, sleep," Pike said. "That's not really likely, is it, Skins? I mean, what if the wolves attack today? Would you want to be sleeping?"

"Honestly?" McConnell asked. "Yes."

"Yeah," Pike said, "me, too, but it's not going to happen."

"I was afraid you were gonna say that."

"Wait a minute," Pike said.

He went behind the bar/counter and into Andrew Locke's back room.

When he came out he said, "One of us can stretch out back there."

At that moment the front door opened and Locke came walking in.

"Look," he said, "do I get to open for business today?"

"Sure," Pike said to him. "Skins, go to sleep in the back and Locke will wake you later."

"What about you?"

"I got an idea last night," Pike said, "and I want to see about it."

"What kind of idea?"

"The kind that might get us more guns."

"That's always a good idea," McConnell said.

"I'll be back later," Pike said. "Explain the set-up to Locke."

"Explain what?" Locke asked. "What set-up?"

Pike patted him on the arm in passing and said, "Skins will explain it."

"Explain what?" Locke asked again as Pike went out the door.

Pike made his way back to the collection of small tents where he'd had his closest encounter with Ol' One-Eye. Looking around, he saw that about half of the tents were inhabited. He started walking around, talking to the men who were renting the tents. What he found was that most of them were passing through, and had no desire to deal themselves into somebody else's hand—especially when there was trouble.

Pike wondered if he'd ever had the same attitude when he was passing through.

He found three men who were interested enough in his proposition to listen.

"What's in it for me?" one of them asked.

"No money, if that's what you mean," Pike said, "but if we can take this wolf down, you'll have a part in it. Ol' One-Eye is almost a legend, and if you—"

"Slow down, Pike," the man said. His name was Tom Harknett. He was tall, well built, and had a likeable manner. "Don't try to do such a great sellin' job on me. You the same Pike used to hang around with Whiskey Sam and Rocky Victor?"

"I've travelled with them, yeah. You know Sam and Rocky?"

"Some," Harknett said. "Enough to hear them talkin' about you. Sure, Pike, I'll lend a hand."

He extended one, as if to seal the deal, and Pike shook it. He told Harknett to meet him at the trading post.

By the time Pike was finished he had three extra guns, and three men who knew how to use them.

He was feeling better about the whole thing.

Before heading back to the trading post Pike decided to stop by Miss Rachel's for a bath, and to see Maria. When he got there, there seemed to be some commotion going on. He saw Miss Rachel standing with some of her girls, who were in various stages of undress. One of them, a tall, buxom, dark-haired girl, was stark naked and apparently thinking nothing of it.

Pike approached them and said, "Is something going on, ladies?"

They looked at him and he saw that several of them were crying.

"I sent for Andy Locke," Miss Rachel said.

"What for?"

"You're Pike, right?" Miss Rachel said.

"That's right."

"Yeah, Maria talked about you. She said you was special."

"Where is Maria?" Pike asked, and one of the girls started crying aloud. A coldness formed in the pit of Pike's stomach.

"Where is she?" he asked again.

"Come with me," Miss Rachel said. "You girls stay here."

Pike followed Miss Rachel as she led him down a blanketed hallway. She stopped in front of a hanging blanket and pointed to it.

"She's in there."

Pike frowned, then pushed the blanket aside and looked inside.

"Oh, Jesus . . ."

Maria was lying half on and half off the bed, her head hanging down. Her face was a mass of blood, which had come from a slit in her throat. The floor beneath her head was a bloody puddle.

"What the hell happened?" he said. He looked at Miss Rachel, who was being careful not to look at Maria. She also wasn't answering him. "I said what the hell happened, damn it?"

Miss Rachel shook her head and said, "I'm waiting for Locke. He's booshway—"

Pike grabbed her by one fat arm and pulled her inside so she could see the body.

"Take a good look, Rachel, and tell me what happened here."

"It was the Frenchman." She was staring at Pike with wide, frightened eyes.

"What? The Frenchman? De Roche?"

"I think that was his name."

"A stocky, dark haired man?"

"Yeah," Rachel said. "He had hair all over his body."

"That's De Roche," Pike said. "He killed her? I thought she wasn't one of your girls?"

"He wanted her," Rachel said. "He said he'd pay double."

"So you gave her to him."

"She didn't want to go. I guess she must have resisted."

"Nobody heard anything?"

"Nothing," she said, shaking her head. "De Roche left, and I didn't go looking for Maria for a couple of hours. By then it was daylight."

Pike shook his head and released her arm.

"Go to the front and wait for Locke."

She nodded and hurried away.

Pike pulled the blanket closed and moved closer to

214

Maria. He knew she was dead, but he checked her anyway.

Red Hawk was right, he thought, angrily. They should have killed De Roche when they had the chance.

When Locke arrived Pike told him what had apparently happened.

"Did anyone see him do it?" Locke asked.

Pike looked at Rachel, who shook her head.

"Just because he was the last man to have her—" Locke started.

"She wasn't one of the girls, Locke," Pike said. "He's the only man who ever paid for her here . . . isn't that right, Rachel?"

"That's right."

"Still," Locke said, "I don't see—has anyone even seen him this morning?"

The girls shook their heads.

"I'll have to ask around, see if anyone has seen him—" Locke started.

"Don't worry, Locke," Pike said. "I'll find him, and when I do you won't have to worry about him."

"Pike, wait—" Locke said as Pike stalked out of the tent. He caught up to him and grabbed his arm.

"Let go!" Pike said, yanking his arm away. Locke shrank back, as if he thought Pike was going to strike him.

"Pike, what about the wolves? Don't forget about the wolves."

"I haven't forgotten, Locke," Pike said. "Go and wake McConnell. Tell him what happened, and that three more men will be coming to the trading post. One of them is named Harknett. Tell Skins I'll talk to him later, and that he should work these three new men into

215

the rotation. Do you understand all of that?"

"Sure, but what about—"

"I'll be by later," Pike said. "First I have to find a skunk, and kill it."

"Pike, if you kill De Roche I'll have to—"

"You'll have to do what?" Pike demanded.

Locke backed off again and said, "Nothing, Pike, nothing at all."

The first place Pike checked was De Roche's old camp, but he wasn't there, and apparently hadn't been there. After that he walked around the settlement, asking people if they had seen him that morning, but nobody had. Pike had to assume that after killing Maria—for whatever reason—De Roche had decided to leave the settlement. Pike couldn't believe that De Roche would give up on the hunt, though, or on collecting the other part of his money. He'd probably come riding back in . . .

Riding . . . that was it. De Roche had to have picked up his horse from Abel.

Pike hurried over to Dom Abel's small stable.

"De Roche?" Abel said. "Sure I saw him today. Came by for his horse, this morning."

"How early?"

"Just after first light."

"Did he say where he was going?"

"Didn't say anything to me," Abel said. "I assumed he was heading out after that wolf."

"You're probably right," Pike said. "Thanks."

"Sure. Is something wrong?"

"Yes," Pike said, and left without explaining it to him.

216

Pike knew that if he found De Roche now he would surely kill him. Afterward, he'd have to deal with the consequences of that. Maybe, then, it was better that he hadn't found him.

Maybe.

He decided to go back to Rachel's to see about burying Maria before he went back to the trading post. He was going to have to control his anger until after they took care of the wolves. There'd be plenty of time to take care of De Roche then.

There was a bitter taste in Pike's mouth, and he knew what it was. It had been in his mouth for all those months it had taken him to find and kill the men who had killed his Crow woman, Sun Rising, months ago.

He had never wanted to taste that again, but now he had it: vengeance. He wished he could spit it out, but he couldn't. There was only one way to get rid of it, and that was to kill De Roche.

Chapter Twenty-Six

When Pike reentered the trading post, McConnell was talking to the three men he had scouted up that morning. He walked to the bar, where Locke was standing.

"Let me have a whiskey, Locke."

"Little early, ain't it, Pike?"

"Just pour it."

Locke poured it and Pike drank it. When he turned around McConnell was approaching him. His friend gave the glass a disapproving look.

"Just one," Pike said, putting the empty glass down on the bar. "How is it going?"

"They're all set. You want to say anything to them?"

Pike rubbed his eyes with the thumb and forefinger of his right hand and said, "No. I'm sure you covered all of it. Just get them out there."

"Right."

McConnell went and spoke to the three men again, and then they filed out. McConnell came back to the bar.

"Sorry you had to get up so quick," Pike said.

"Forget it. Locke told me what happened. Did you find him?"

"No," Pike said. "He collected his horse early this morning and rode out."

"Going after him?" McConnell asked.

Pike looked at his friend. He recognized the disapproving tone in his friend's voice. He had heard it for months. Skins McConnell did not approve of revenge. He thought it was a waste of time.

"Eventually," Pike said. "Want to try and argue me out of it?"

"Nope," McConnell said, "not me."

Pike shook his head and looked at something over his friend's head.

"Red Hawk was right."

"About killin' De Roche?"

"Yeah."

"No," McConnell said, "he wasn't—not at the time, anyway. It seems that way now, but it wasn't at the time."

"If we had killed him, that girl would be alive."

"Locke told me no one saw him do it," McConnell said. "You gonna condemn the man without evidence?"

"No," Pike said, "I'm not going to condemn him, I'm going to send him to hell, where he belongs."

"Well," McConnell said, "I might try to argue you out of that . . . when the time comes. We've got somethin' else to take care of first, right?"

"Right," Pike said.

That seemed to satisfy McConnell, for the moment.

"Why don't you get yourself some sleep in the back room and I'll go outside."

"Yeah," Pike said, "yeah, maybe I will."

After McConnell left, Pike went into the back room and tried to make himself comfortable. After a half an hour he knew there was no way he was going to be able to fall asleep.

As he came out of the back room Locke hastened to get out of his way. Pike left the trading post and went to see how Jean and Barry Windham were doing.

Jean stepped out of the tent to talk to Pike.

"You look terrible," she said to him, immediately. "Has something happened?"

"Nothing to concern you," he said. "Nothing about the wolves. Oh, I've got three extra men, now. When the pack comes we should be able to handle them."

"I hope so."

"How is he?"

"He hasn't opened his eyes at all, and he seems to be dreaming. He's having bad dreams, Pike, and you're in them."

"Me?"

"He's called for two people in his sleep," she said. "His father . . . and you."

Pike frowned.

"If it's a bad dream he must be dreaming about the wolf."

"Yes."

Pike rubbed his eyes again. They felt grainy, and there was a dull throb behind them.

"What's wrong?" she asked, touching his arm. "What's happened?"

He told her about Maria being killed, describing the girl as a friend.

"She wasn't one of Rachel's whores."

"I remember her," Jean said. "She had a scar on her face, didn't she?"

"She had a scar," he said, "and it ran much deeper than her face."

"I'm sorry she's dead," she said. "Who killed her?"

"De Roche."

221

"The man the settlement hired to hunt the wolf?"

"That's right."

"Will you . . . go after him?"

"Yes," he said, "after we get the wolf."

"You look like you need some rest," she said, "or you won't be going after anyone, or anything. Why don't you go to my house?"

"Your house?"

"You can sleep in my bed and no one will bother you there."

"I have to be around, in case the wolves come," he said, "but I appreciate the offer, Jean."

"Well," she said, "maybe in the future, when this is all done and you want to get a good night's sleep."

"Yes," he said, "in the future. I'll check back with you later to see how Barry is."

"All right."

De Roche was angry. He wasn't angry with himself, though, he was angry with the girl. If she had just done what he wanted he wouldn't have gotten angry and she wouldn't be dead. In De Roche's mind, the girl had killed herself.

Still, he'd have to explain what happened, but he was smart enough to know that it would be easier on him if he could kill the wolf, first. He was damned sure that the whole settlement would willingly trade a scar-faced little whore for the death of Ol' One-Eye.

De Roche was astride his horse, where he was determined to stay for the entire day. The wolf pack was coming today, of that he was sure, and he wanted to be ready for them—that is, ready for their leader. While the fools in the settlement were trying to shoot up the pack, he intended to turn the pack by firing one well-placed shot at Ol' One-Eye. Once he killed the wolf and saved the settlement, the death of a whore would be insignificant.

Ol' One-Eye was ready. It was time to lead the pack to their feeding, and the pack was more than ready, they were eager.

Chapter Twenty-Seven

Pike made one circuit of the settlement, checking on the positions of the men, and then went back to the trading post. McConnell was there, working on a beer with Locke behind the bar.

"Business is lousy," Locke said as Pike entered. "I should be charging you fellas for your beer."

"Wolves will do that to business," McConnell said. "Most of the people are staying indoors."

"Everyone at the tent camp has their fires going high," Pike said.

"That's not gonna help them," McConnell said. "Not against a pack of wolves that will come right into a warm camp."

"Well, I hope this is all over after today," Locke said.

"I have a feeling it will be," Pike said. "In fact, Skins, if the pack doesn't come by midday I think we should get all of the men outside and keep them ready."

McConnell nodded.

"Yep, if they're not here by midday it's almost sure they'll attack before dark tonight."

"How can you be so sure?" Locke asked.

"The pack has to be hungry," Pike said. "I don't think even Ol' One-Eye could keep them from attacking tonight."

"One of us better go and talk to Dom Abel," McConnell said. "He's got the most livestock in one place."

"Good point," Pike said. "I'll go over and talk to him. I was sort of short with him, this morning."

"I'll stay here," McConnell said.

Pike nodded and left, and walked over to Dom Abel's little stable. From what he could see Abel had a half a dozen horses and at least that many mules packed into a leanto that probably would have more comfortably accommodated three of each.

"Can I do something for you?" Abel asked.

"Yeah," Pike said, "I wanted to apologize for the way I talked to you this morning."

"Forget it," Abel said, "you looked pretty upset about something."

Briefly, Pike told Abel about the murder of Maria, which had probably been committed by De Roche.

"Well, I can see why you were upset," Abel said. "I appreciate you coming to explain it to me, though."

"Well, I really came over to warn you," Pike said. "We're expecting the wolf pack to hit the settlement today, and you have the most livestock collected in one place."

"I'm glad you mentioned it," Abel said. "I'll be on the lookout."

"Can I send a man over here to keep a watch for you?" Pike asked.

"No," Abel said, "I have a couple of rifles and a pistol, and I know how to use them."

"Well, I'd keep them close at all times, if I was you," Pike said.

"I intend to."

Pike started to walk away, but stopped short when something occurred to him.

"Uh, when the pack does come in, if you hear some

commotion I'd stay right here instead of running to see if you can help."

"Look after myself, you mean?"

"I mean look after the livestock you've been charged with," Pike said. "I assume most of these animals belong to other people than yourself."

"You're right about that," Abel said. "I appreciate you coming over."

"I just hope we all get through this in one piece," Pike said.

"I hope you get that big gray wolf," Abel said, "the one that injured the boy."

"I'm going to try my damndest."

As Pike walked away he couldn't help thinking that if he had his horse in Abel's stable he'd go and get it and guard it himself. As it stood, he and McConnell had their horses behind Locke's trading post.

Pike was glad he wasn't the type of guy who named his horses, and became attached to them. If his horse became food for the wolves, he'd be able to shrug it off and get himself another one.

When he got back to the trading post McConnell wasn't there.

"Where's Skins?"

"He said he'd be right back. I think he was going over to Miss Rachel's."

Pike assumed McConnell wanted to check on his friend, Mathilda.

"Hey, Locke, you've got a back door, don't you?" Pike asked.

Warily, Locke said, "Yeah. So?"

"Would a horse fit through it?"

227

"What?"

"I was just thinking, if Skins and I brought our horses inside, we wouldn't have to worry about losing them to the wolf pack."

"What? Bring your horses *inside?*"

"I mean, if we lose our animals in defense of the settlement," Pike added, "we'd expect the settlement to replace them."

Locke frowned now, wondering which was the lesser of two evils.

"Thanks, Locke," Pike said, "I'm going in the back to bring the horses in."

As Pike came around the bar Locke was muttering, "Horses in my store. What's gonna be next?"

Pike went in the back and walked his and McConnell's horses into Locke's back room. Their saddles and gear were already there, and he started moving things around to accommodate the girth of the horses.

Locke was watching from the door, a pained look on his face.

"Relax, Locke," Pike said, "it's likely to be just for one day."

"Can't you put something under them?" Locke complained. "I don't need horseshit on my floor."

Pike slapped Locke on the shoulder and said, "Take it easy, nobody's going to be here to smell it."

"Don't remind me."

McConnell's intention had been to stop in and see if Mathilda was all right, in the face of one of the girls being murdered. Not to mention the threat of attack by wolves. Mathilda, however, had other ideas.

She pulled McConnell into her little blanketed

228

cubbyhole and had his clothes off before he knew it. Naked, armed with a huge erection, he watched from her bed as she peeled off her clothes. She was tall and slender, and the hair between her legs was red. She had small breasts and long, long legs, and as she joined him on the bed he could smell her various scents: perfume, sweat and sex, all of which were stimulating.

She climbed astride him, pinning his erection between them, and lay down with her head on his chest.

That was when she told him that *she* had been with De Roche before Maria had, and she was still scared because it could just as well been her he killed as Maria.

"You were with De Roche?"

"Yes."

"Did he have a knife when you were with him?"

She thought a moment.

"There was a knife, but he never showed it to me. It was on the floor with his other gear."

"Was he abusive?"

She laughed against his chest and said, "What's abusive? He wanted me to do things, and I did them. They weren't things I would normally have done."

He put his arms around her and she lifted her head and kissed the hollow of his throat. She started to kiss his chest, then worked her way downward, running her tongue over his belly, and then she swooped down on her ultimate goal and captured it in her hot mouth.

There was very little talk after that . . .

Later, as McConnell dressed, he asked Mathilda who else had been with De Roche.

"Before me he had Barbara."

McConnell went to talk to Barbara, a big, busty, big-hipped woman with dark hair who had been a whore for more than half of her life.

"He was scary, that's for sure," Barbara said. "When we were finished he pinched my tit hard and left a bruise, but he never threatened me with a knife."

She shivered then, rubbing her upper arms.

"Jesus, it gives me the chills. He coulda killed me instead of Maria." Her eyes widened then and she said, "You don't think he'll come back, do you?"

"Don't worry," McConnell said, "if he does come back I know someone who will make sure he never comes here."

When McConnell returned to the trading post he told Pike what Mathilda had told him.

"But he never threatened her with the knife?"

"No."

Pike frowned.

McConnell said, "That makes me wonder what would have made him show the knife to Maria?"

"Obviously," Pike said, "Maria would not do the things the other girls would do."

"Yeah, but he wasn't even drinking," McConnell said. "What would make a man do something like that?"

"He'd have to be crazy," Andy Locke said from behind the bar. Locke was wrinkling his nose. Did he smell horseshit?

Pike looked from Locke to McConnell, then back to Locke.

"Andy," he said, "have a beer on me."

"Hey, thanks," Locke said, before he realized that he wasn't charging Pike for his beer.

Chapter Twenty-Eight

De Roche saw them.

Below him he saw ten wolves, nine in the pack and the leader with the silver back—Ol' One-Eye. They appeared to be heading straight for the settlement. Luckily, he was downwind of them and they did not smell him.

He raised his rifle to his shoulder and sighted down the barrel . . . then paused. If he shot the wolf now, the pack would scatter. If he waited until the wolves were inside the settlement and then killed Ol' One-Eye, the people would be much more appreciative. Also, if he let the wolves get inside, maybe one of them would take care of Pike or McConnell for him.

Actually, if De Roche hadn't killed the girl he would have shot the wolf right then and there, but he needed the wolves to make people forget about the girl.

He lowered the rifle and decided to simply follow the pack into the settlement and see what transpired.

Pike saw the doctor walking toward the tent where the Windhams were, and moved to intercept him.

"Doctor, my name is Pike. I'm a friend of the Windhams. How is Barry doing?"

"Better than I am," the man said. He appeared to be in late forties, a slightly-built man under six feet, with a very pale complexion. "I have patients waiting for me back home. I'll be heading back there as soon as the boy is out of danger, or . . ."

"Or what?"

"Well," the doctor said, "let's just say when he's out of danger, one way or another."

"You mean he could still die?"

"Mr. Pike," the doctor said, "to be perfectly honest, I'm surprised he didn't die a long time ago. There is something keeping that boy alive that I just can't identify."

"Maybe it's just a strong will to live."

"An extremely strong will, for one so young," the doctor said. "If you'll excuse me, I'd like to check on him."

"Maybe I'll walk with you—" Pike started to say, but suddenly he heard someone calling his name.

"Pike!"

He looked up and saw Willie McGee running toward him.

"Don't let me keep you, Doctor."

The doctor continued on and Pike walked toward McGee.

"They're here," McGee said. "The pack is coming."

"Are you sure?"

"I saw them," McGee said, "I saw *something* coming down the hill."

"Come on," Pike said. He wanted to check for himself before starting a panic.

De Roche sat astride his horse at the top of the hill, watching the wolves go down. They still had not smelled him, or if they had, were ignoring him in favor

232

of what they could get in the settlement.

He could make out two men running toward the hill, and one of them looked large enough to be Pike.

He smiled and, having given the wolves enough of a head start, started down the hill himself.

Pike stared up at the hill and before long saw some shapes moving down.

"Willie, go and sound the alarm. Get everyone who has a rifle out here. We might be able to stop them before they even get inside the settlement."

"Right."

As the younger man ran off, Pike looked farther up the hill and saw the man on the horse.

De Roche, following the pack down.

"Sonofabitch."

Between the base of the hill and the settlement there was a large expanse of ground that the pack would have to cross. Hopefully, while they were out in the open they would be able to kill most of them—depending on how well the other men could shoot.

Pike turned when he heard the men running up behind him, led by McConnell. Counting Pike and McConnell, they had ten men with rifles. Pike knew he and McConnell could shoot, and the three men he had drafted from the tent camp probably could, too. That meant that at least half of them could shoot. If any of the others could, as well, that would be a bonus.

"Fan out!" Pike shouted as the men reached him.

"Where are they?" McConnell asked.

"Coming down the hill, almost to the bottom. Keep looking, you'll spot them from time to time, moving between the trees."

"I just saw one."

"Look farther up."

McConnell did, and saw the rider.

"De Roche?" he asked.

"It's got to be."

"He's just following the pack in, then," McConnell said.

"I'll save a shot for him," Pike said.

McConnell didn't comment.

Pike looked up and down the line. The people from the settlement were nervously handling their guns, while the other men were simply holding firm and waiting.

"Skins, make sure the settlement people don't fire until we give the word."

"Right."

McConnell ran down the line to relay the message, and then returned to Pike's side.

"You and I will take the big one in front," Pike said. "If we can kill Ol' One-Eye, the others might just scatter."

"I doubt it," McConnell said. "At this point, if they're hungry enough, the smell of the livestock will keep them coming."

"You're probably right."

"Here they come!" Harknett shouted.

Sure enough, there were some wolves crossing the ground between the hill and the settlement.

"Something's wrong," McConnell said.

"I know," Pike said, "I don't see Ol' One-Eye."

"And that can't be the whole pack."

"Maybe that's all that's left."

They suspended conversation as the pack came closer and closer.

"Steady," Pike loudly. "If we fire too soon they'll just scatter back into the hills. Let's wait until they're closer to us than they are to the trees."

Pike watched the wolves carefully, and when he was

234

sure they had passed the mid-point he shouted, "Fire!"

The men fired, and then those who had pistols took them out and fired as well. The others hurriedly reloaded, and then fired again.

"Let's get closer," Pike said after he and McConnell had reloaded.

They started forward, and the other men followed. They all fired again, some falling to one knee to steady their rifles. For the amount of shooting that was being done, Pike was assuming that most of the settlement men were missing. As far as Pike could see it was he, McConnell, Harknett, and Willie McGee who were doing the most effective shooting.

Suddenly, there was no movement ahead of them.

"Hold your fire!" Pike called.

He and McConnell moved forward and encountered the carcass of a dead wolf, and then another. They nudged the bodies, making sure they were dead, then kept moving. They found a third wolf, and then a fourth, and then could not find any more.

"This is not right," Pike said. "There's only four wolves."

"And where's De Roche?"

"Good question," Pike said. The Frenchman was nowhere to be found.

"He's baited us," McConnell said.

"You're right," Pike said. "That cunning devil has taken the rest of the pack to another point, probably the north side."

"Abel's stable," McConnell said, quickly. "You said yourself he's got the most livestock in one place."

"We'd better get over there fast," Pike said. "He's all alone."

As he said that, they heard the shots from the direction of Abel's stable.

De Roche was filled with admiraton for the pack leader. The animal was sacrificing four of his wolves to keep the men busy, and took the other five around the settlement with him to enter from another point.

De Roche followed.

Pike left four men behind, just in case Ol' One-Eye doubled back on them again. He took the other men with him through the settlement, where people were peering out of their homes to see what the shooting was.

"Stay inside!" Pike shouted, and the people withdrew, most of them women.

As they ran past the tent where the Windhams and the doctor was Jean Windham stepped outside.

"Jean, get back inside!"

"Did you get him?"

Pike waved at her and kept running, hoping that would answer her question. He also hoped that she would obey him and go inside.

Pike had the longest legs, and Willie McGee was the youngest, so they were out ahead of the rest of the men, and reached the leanto first.

"Jesus," McGee said.

The leanto had been knocked down, and several animals were on the ground, either dead or injured. Many of them had fled, probably chased by the wolves.

"There!" McGee said.

As he said it a wolf looked up from the carcass of a horse, its muzzle dripping with blood. It was big and gray, but it had two eyes. It stared at the two of them and growled.

236

Pike lifted his rifle and fired, sending a ball into the wolf's head.

The others caught up and stopped short, surveying the carnage.

"Jesus Christ," one of them said.

"Where's Abel?" McConnell said.

"Good question," Pike said.

They all stood in silence while a couple of men checked beneath the rubble of the leanto. They discovered the carcass of a mule, but there was not a man under there.

"He's not there," Kevin Mack said.

"All right," Pike said, "everybody reload. We're going to have to split up and hunt these beasts down. They're probably trying to chase down the livestock, but if they come across another likely victim, they won't hesitate. In a feeding frenzy, they'll attack anyone or anything that looks weak."

"Like a child," Mack said.

"Exactly," Pike said. "Split up by twos, and if you see anyone outdoors who shouldn't be there, get them back inside."

"Don't fire together," McConnell added. "Know who's going to fire, and who's going to reload, so you're never empty at the same time."

"McGee," Pike said, "you're with me. Let's move out."

Chapter Twenty-Nine

Pike and McGee walked over to the tent camp to see if anyone had encountered any wolves, or if they had seen Dom Abel. When they reached there they were surprised by what they saw.

Many of the tents had fallen, or were knocked down. Some of the fires had been trampled out, and there was no one around.

"They were through here, all right," Pike said, looking around.

"How many more are there?" McGee asked.

"Couldn't be more than half a dozen."

"And they did this?"

"One wolf is enough to cause a panic, Willie," Pike said. "Imagine what half a dozen can do."

"I see what they can do."

Pike's eyes fell on the tent that he and Ol' One-Eye had shared briefly. He wondered idly if the wolf was in there now.

"There could be a wolf in any of these tents," he said to McGee.

"Are you serious?" McGee asked.

Pike thought a moment, then said, "No. Come on, let's keep looking."

It was McConnell and Kevin Mack who walked out toward Jean Windham's house.

"Look," Mack said.

McConnell saw that the front door was open.

"Let's take a look."

They walked to the house, rifles held at the ready. When they reached the door they found that it was not just open, but that it had been forced open.

"I'll go first," McConnell said, and Mack nodded.

McConnell stepped into the house and stopped when he saw that it was in a shambles. From behind him, Mack stuck his head in.

"Oh, my God," he said. "The wolves were here."

"Not the pack," McConnell said, looking around, "just one."

Amid the debris was a large, steaming pile of shit.

"Why would a wolf do this?" Mack asked.

"This particular wolf," McConnell said, "seems to have a fascination for this particular family."

"Why?"

"I don't know," McConnell said, "but we'd better go and check on them."

They got out of the house and started toward the center of the settlement.

Pike and McGee walked the woods behind the tent camp and found nothing but tracks, and headed back toward the settlement.

"Where could those men have run to?" McGee asked.

"I don't know," Pike said. "It's awfully quiet around here for a settlement with wolves loose in it."

"Yeah," McGee said, "why?"

Before Pike could answer there was a shot, followed by another.

"The wolves?" Mack asked.

"Or a couple of your people shooting at each other," Pike said. "Let's go have a look. Sounded like it came from the settlement."

They started running and had gone a hundred yards when McGee suddenly tripped over something and went sprawling onto the ground. Pike turned and walked back to see what had happened.

"What'd I trip over?" McGee asked, crawling to his feet.

"A body."

"Whose?"

"He's pretty well chewed up," Pike said, "but from the way he's built, the big belly and the white hair, I'd say we've found Dom Abel."

"Jesus," McGee said, "he sure is chewed up, ain't he?"

"Look around."

"For what?"

"His guns," Pike said. "He said he had three guns, two rifles and a pistol. He must have gotten off a shot."

They searched the area, and while they were doing so heard several shots from different locations.

"The place must be crawling with wolves," McGee said.

"Maybe," Pike said, "but where the hell is the big one? Where's the leader? That's what I want to know. Come on, let's head back."

They started back to the settlement again and again they heard a flurry of shots.

"Jesus," Pike said, shaking his head, "these guys are shooting at shadows."

241

When Pike and McGee reached the settlement they spotted McConnell and Mack. They stopped and compared notes.

So far they knew that the wolves had run through Dom Abel's stable, the tent camp, and at least one wolf had invaded the Windham home.

"Ol' One-Eye," Pike said. "What other wolf would do that?"

"No other one would have a reason, I guess," McConnell said.

"What are you sayin'? That there's a wolf with a reason to go after the Windham family? Don't wolves attack just to eat?"

"Normally," Pike said. "We'd better check on Jean and Barry."

"That's what we were about to do," McConnell said.

On the way to the tent Pike told McConnell about finding Abel's body. There were still occasional shots from the distance.

"I hope some of those shots are being fired at wolves," Pike said.

De Roche was riding with his head down, following the tracks in the ground. He couldn't understand how he had lost the big wolf. He'd been right behind them all the way, and then he was gone—they were *all* gone. The tracks were still there, but the wolves were gone.

Where the hell was the big, one-eyed wolf.

Suddenly, without warning, something struck him on the back, knocking him from his horse. He hit the ground hard, the wind rushing from his lungs. He tried to roll over, but suddenly there was thick, warm fur in his face. He reached out with his hands to push it away, but before he could, sharp teeth clamped down on his throat. He felt the skin break, he felt the blood flow,

242

and he wished he'd shot this damn wolf when he had the chance . . .

Over and over again the wolf attacked his father, and over and over Pike stepped out of the woods and raised his rifle, but he never fired it.

Fire the rifle, Barry wanted to shout, fire it!

And then the dream changed.

Suddenly, the wolf left his father on the ground, turned and started walking toward him. Still, Pike pointed his gun and didn't fire.

Abruptly, the wolf changed direction and started running. Barry looked that way and saw that the animal was running toward his mother.

No, he wanted to shout, Mom, but nothing would come out. He tried to move, but he couldn't.

He kept trying to move.

When they reached the tent Pike went inside to see Jean Windham. When he entered he saw that Barry Windham was thrashing about on the bed.

"Jean!"

Jean was standing away from the bed, staring at her son.

"He knows, Pike," she said, staring at Pike with haunted eyes, "he knows that the wolf is here."

"Jean . . . how could he know?"

"I don't know, but you have to kill it," she cried out. "You have to. If you don't, my son is going to die."

"Jean . . . what do you mean?" He walked over to her and took her by the shoulders.

"I don't know," she said, "I just know that if you don't kill the wolf, Barry will die."

"All right," he said, moving toward the door. "All

right, and I'll find the doctor and send him over."

Outside he said to McGee and Mack, "You fellas go and find the doctor and get him over here. Skins, you and I have to find that wolf."

"What's wrong?" McConnell asked, trying to keep up with Pike.

"I don't know," Pike said. "The boy's thrashing around on the bed, and Jean is convinced that if we don't kill the wolf, the boy will die."

"You mean, the wolf will kill him?"

"No," Pike said, "no, she made it sound like he would just . . . die if we didn't kill the wolf."

"How could that happen?"

"I don't know," Pike said, "all I know is that we've got to find that wolf and kill it."

"Well then, let's do it," McConnell said. "We'll leave the other wolves to the others."

"Yeah," Pike said, "if they don't shoot each other first."

Ol' One-Eye pulled his snout out of the bloody hollow of De Roche's throat. He licked his muzzle and shook his head. The blood was warm and sweet, but it wasn't what he wanted.

He had been to the Windham house, looking for Windham blood. He had only attacked De Roche because he recognized the threat that the man posed to him. There were other men, too, who were a threat to him, but he would kill them also, if they got in his way.

He lifted his nose and sniffed the air. Finding the scent he wanted he slunk into the trees and started to work his way around to a point where he could see the center of the settlement. From cover he could see what he wanted to see.

The big tent, where the Windhams were.

244

To get to it he would have to run across open ground. Before he did that, he had to make sure that the men with guns were otherwise occupied.

"Wait a minute," Pike said, some time later.

"What?"

Pike stopped walking and shook his head.

"What we've been doing here," he said, as if he couldn't believe it himself, "is we've been getting outsmarted by a wolf."

McConnell waited for more, and when it wasn't forthcoming he said, "Yeah? So?"

"Skins, we've been *letting* ourselves be outsmarted by a wolf."

"So tell me how we stop doing that?"

"We stop taking this thing so personally."

McConnell gave Pike a look and said, "Ain't that what I been tryin' to tell you all along?"

"Yes, it is," Pike said, "and why didn't you try harder?"

"Why didn't I—"

"Look," Pike said, "this wolf has us running around chasing our tails."

"Yeah?"

"What we've got to do is sit down and wait for him to come to us."

"And just where do you suggest we do this sitting?" McConnell asked.

"Come with me," Pike said, "and I'll tell you."

Chapter Thirty

They camped in front of the big tent. Inside, Pike could still hear Barry moving around on the bed. The doctor was with him, but didn't know what was going on.

"It's like he's having a dream," the doctor had said.

"A bad dream?" Pike asked.

"The worst."

"What about what Mrs. Windham said?"

"That sounds like hysteria, to me," the doctor said, and walked off.

"Yeah, well," Pike said, "not to me."

Pike and McConnell stood outside the tent, listening to the shooting in the distance. It was closing in on evening, and every so often one or two of the men would come by and report that they'd shot a wolf.

Mack and McGee were approaching, and if they reported shooting a wolf, that would leave only Ol' One-Eye.

"Get one?" Pike asked.

"No," McGee said.

"So there's still two left," McConnell said. "Ol' One-Eye and one of his pack."

"You won't have to worry about De Roche anymore," Kevin Mack said.

"Why not?" Pike asked.

"We found him," Willie McGee said. "His throat was torn out."

Pike looked at McConnell with raised eyebrows.

"Looks like Ol' One-Eye saved you the trouble," McConnell said.

"Have you seen him?" McGee asked.

"No," Pike said, "but I'll bet he can see us."

McGee and Mack started to look around.

"Hey, hey," Pike said, "there's another wolf out there."

They all heard a shot from a distance.

"We know," McGee said.

"Well, go and get it."

"Sure you wouldn't like us to stay here with you?" McGee asked.

Pike jerked his head toward McConnell and said, "I've already got a baby sitter."

Mack nodded and pulled McGee by the arm.

"He's out there," Pike said. "I can feel him watching us."

"Yeah?" McConnell said. "Well, I'm glad I can't."

Ol' One-Eye watched the two men in front of the tent. His nose told him that the prey he wanted was inside the tent, but to get to them he was going to have to move fast. Very fast.

"Pike."

"What?"

"What's that?"

"What's what?"

"That, that, that," McConnell shouted pointing straight ahead.

Pike looked and saw something running toward them. Something big, something fast, and something gray.

"Jesus, it's him, it's him," Pike said.

"Let's get 'im," McConnell said.

They both raised their rifles.

"Me first," Pike said, and fired.

Ol' One-Eye jerked, but kept coming.

"Jesus, I hit him," Pike said, reloading, "I know I did."

"My turn," McConnell said, and fired. This time Ol' One-Eye jerked almost sideways, righted himself, and kept coming.

"I hit 'im, too," McConnell said, reloading. "Damn, he's still comin'."

Jean Windham stuck her head out of the tent.

"What's happening?"

"Get back inside, Jean," Pike said, "and take this." He pulled his Kentucky pistol from his belt and handed it to her.

"Pike—"

"Get back inside and stay by Barry."

When Jean went back inside, Barry was sitting up in bed, his eyes open.

"Barry!"

"Kill him," Barry said, his eyes wild. "Kill him."

His eyes were open, but Jean knew that Barry couldn't see her.

"Pike!" she shouted. "You've got to kill it . . . kill it now!"

*　　　*　　　*

249

Outside Pike aimed and fired.

"Damn, I know I hit him, but he's still coming!"

"Three times," McConnell said. "What's it take to kill this sonofabitch?"

"Pike!" Jean shouted from inside.

"Skins," Pike said, "we'll just have to wait for him to reach us."

"Hit him at point blank range?"

"That's it."

"All right," McConnell said. "Are you reloaded?"

"I am."

They both fell to one knee and waited, watching Ol' One-Eye close the ground.

As the animal came closer Pike could see that it was bleeding, and yet he was still coming, every stride as strong as the one before.

"Wait . . ." Pike said, "wait . . ."

"I am waiting," McConnell said.

Ol' One-Eye came closer . . . and closer . . . until they could almost smell him . . . until he was almost on top of them . . .

"Now!"

Pike fired, and McConnell a split second later. The lead balls pounded into Ol' One-Eye, flinging him sideways and to the ground.

"He's down," McConnell said.

"But is he dead?"

"Why don't you go and see?"

"Why don't you go?" Pike said.

"Why don't we reload?"

"Good damned idea."

As the both started to reload, Ol' One-Eye got up and started for them at full speed.

"Jesus . . ." Pike said.

"Christ . . ." McConnell said.

"Die!" Jean Windham said, and fired the Kentucky pistol.

The ball struck Ol' One-Eye right in his good eye and penetrated to his brain, lodging there. He had launched himself in a jump just before she fired, and his momentum carried him into both Pike and McConnell, knocking them to the ground with Ol' One-Eye's carcass on top of them.

"Momma . . ." Barry Windham called from inside.

Epilogue

Pike and McConnell rode into the Snake camp, attracting the eyes of everyone. By the time they reached the center of the camp Red Hawk had come out of his teepee and was waiting for them. Next to him was a tall, beautiful Snake woman.

Pike rode right up to Red Hawk and allowed the carcass of Ol' One-Eye to slide from his saddle. It struck the ground with a loud thud.

Red Hawk leaned over to examine the carcass and make sure it was the right wolf.

He smiled when he saw where the fatal wound was.

"You killed him," Red Hawk said.

"No," Pike said, "a woman killed him."

Red Hawk raised his eyebrows.

"The child's mother?"

"Yes."

"It is fitting."

"Yes."

"He's gone now, Red Hawk," Pike said.

"Yes, he is," Red Hawk said. "My only source of fear, and he is gone now."

"Yeah, well," Pike said, "it's a funny thing about what scares us."

"What is that?"

"We always manage to find something else."

Red Hawk thought that over and then said, "Yes."

Pike reached down with his hand and Red Hawk stepped forward and took it.

"The carcass is yours," Pike said. "A gift. Do something with it."

Red Hawk's wife stepped forward, took her husband's arm and said, "I will make a headdress of it."

Pike smiled and said, "I'd like to come back and see that some time."

"You can come back," Red Hawk said. "He-Whose-Head-Touches-The-Sky is always welcome."

Pike nodded, McConnell lifted his hand in a wave that Red Hawk returned, and then they turned and rode out.

EDGE by George G. Gilman

#5 BLOOD ON SILVER (17-225, $3.50)
The Comstock Lode was one of the richest silver strikes the
world had ever seen. So Edge was there. So was the Tabor
gang—sadistic killers led by a renegade Quaker. The volup-
tuous Adele Firman, a band of brutal Shoshone Indians,
and an African giant were there, too. Too bad. They
learned that gold may be warm but silver is death. They
didn't live to forget Edge.

#6 RED RIVER (17-226, $3.50)
In jail for a killing he didn't commit, Edge is puzzled by
the prisoner in the next cell. Where had they met before?
Was it at Shiloh, or in the horror of Andersonville?

This is the sequel to KILLER'S BREED, an earlier volume
in this series. We revisit the bloody days of the Civil War
and incredible scenes of cruelty and violence as our young
nation splits wide open, blue armies versus gray armies,
tainting the land with a river of blood. And Edge was
there.

*Available wherever paperbacks are sold, or order direct from the
Publisher. Send cover price plus 50¢ per copy for mailing and
handling to Pinnacle Books, Dept.17-530, 475 Park Avenue
South, New York, N.Y. 10016. Residents of New York, New Jer-
sey and Pennsylvania must include sales tax. DO NOT SEND
CASH.*

THE DESTROYER by Warren Murphy & Richard Sapir